"But you sav

"You actually thre___ ___ ___ ___ gun. How can I ever repay you for that?" Jo exclaimed, her face paper-pale and her gray eyes dark with disbelief and emotion.

Gavin pulled his sweater over his head and Jo winced at the sight of the wound in his upper arm. But she immediately pulled off her top, which she ripped into strips with her teeth and fingernails then applied as a pad and pressure bandages to his wound.

Gavin Hastings flinched, but there was a suggestion of humor in his eyes as they rested on her, her upper body clad only in a bra, as she worked on the dressings.

"What can you do to repay me, Jo? I think it would be a damn good idea if you married me." He swayed suddenly, and blacked out.

LINDSAY ARMSTRONG was born in South Africa, but now lives in Australia with her New Zealand–born husband and their five children. They have lived in nearly every state of Australia and have tried their hand at some unusual, for them, occupations, such as farming and horse training—all grist to the mill for a writer! Lindsay started writing romances when her youngest child began school and she was left feeling at a loose end. She is still doing it and loving it.

THE MILLIONAIRE'S MARRIAGE CLAIM

LINDSAY ARMSTRONG

THE MILLIONAIRE AFFAIR

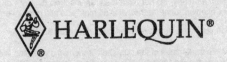

HARLEQUIN®

TORONTO • NEW YORK • LONDON
AMSTERDAM • PARIS • SYDNEY • HAMBURG
STOCKHOLM • ATHENS • TOKYO • MILAN • MADRID
PRAGUE • WARSAW • BUDAPEST • AUCKLAND

ISBN 0-373-82028-3

THE MILLIONAIRE'S MARRIAGE CLAIM

First North American Publication 2005.

Copyright © 2005 by Lindsay Armstrong.

This edition published by arrangement with Harlequin Books S.A.

www.eHarlequin.com

Printed in U.S.A.

CHAPTER ONE

JOANNE LUCAS steered her grey Range Rover over the appalling road and shook her head.

Sure, she hadn't expected the drive to a sheep station somewhere south of Charleville in outback Queensland to be a picnic. But the road had been quite good until she'd turned off onto the station track, and it was far worse than anything she'd anticipated. It was also quite a bit further than she'd expected to drive, and the chill dusk of a winter's evening was drawing in.

She scanned the horizon for some sign of habitation but there was none. This was serious sheep country, the Murweh shire—she knew from the research she'd done it carried approximately eight hundred thousand head of them! There were also cattle stations in the area so you expected it to be wide open and isolated.

On the other hand, her destination, Kin Can station, had quite a reputation. So did its owners, the Hastings family, for wealth and excellence in the wool they bred.

How come they couldn't afford to put in a decent road to the homestead, then? And how on earth did the wool trucks cope with it?

Come to think of it, if she hadn't had her wits about her, she would have missed the small, nearly illegible Kin Can sign on a gate—another surprise because

5

she'd been led to believe the station was well sign-posted.

Do they actively discourage visitors? she asked herself, then slammed on the brakes as she topped a rise to see a man standing in the middle of the track aiming a gun at her.

Do they ever! It flashed through her mind, followed immediately by—So what to do now?

Any decision was taken out of her hands as the man loped forward and wrenched her door open before she could lock it. Not only that, he slung the gun over his shoulder and manhandled her out onto the road.

'Now look here,' she began, 'this is insane and—'

'What's your name?' he barked at her as he backed her up against the bonnet.

'Jo…Joanne, b-but people call me Jo,' she stammered.

'Just as I thought, although I was expecting a Joe—of the masculine variety—but perhaps they thought you could seduce me and keep doing it until they tracked me down.'

He paused and a flash of ironic amusement lit his intensely blue eyes as he looked her up and down then murmured, 'On the other hand, you don't look that feminine, Jo, so I'll go with my first scenario.'

Jo, who had gasped several times as he'd spoken, lost her temper and stamped heavily on his toe with the heel of her booted foot.

He didn't even flinch. 'Steel toecaps, darlin',' he drawled. 'So it gets your goat up to be called unfeminine?'

Jo breathed heavily but a small portion of her mind

conceded that, yes, it had—which was just about as insane as the whole mad situation. Nor could she resist a glance downwards, although she did resist the urge to tell this crazy person that most women would look unfeminine in creased cargo pants, a bulky anorak and a knitted beanie that concealed her hair.

She did quell the sneaky little voice in her head that reminded her some men found her height and straight shoulders unfeminine anyway...

'Look here, whoever you are,' she began, 'I'm expected up at the homestead so—'

'I'll bet you are, Jo,' he rasped, 'but we're going a different way. Let's just see what you're packing first.' He started to pat her down like a policeman.

'Packing?' It came out in a strangled way edged with outrage as she tried to evade his hands. 'Will you stop touching me? I'm not packing anything.'

'Take 'em off, then,' he ordered as his hands reached her waist.

Jo gaped at him. 'Take what off?'

'Your strides, lady.'

'I most certainly will not—are you out of your mind?'

'OK! Turn round and lean over the bonnet so I can search for hip holsters, thigh holsters or wherever women carry their concealed weapons.'

Jo stared at him in the fading daylight and wondered if she was the one going mad or—was this a nightmare? But the substance of her nightmare was anything but dream-like.

He was tall, taller than she was, with good shoulders. In a navy jumper and torn, dirty jeans, he looked to be extremely fit in a lean, rangy way. His thick black hair was short and ruffled and his jaw was covered with black stubble. Then there were those furious blue eyes that gave every indication of a man not to be trifled with.

But why? How? What? she wondered wildly. Some modern day bushranger on the loose? Surely not!

It's not unheard of, she corrected herself immediately, but why would he have been expecting any kind of a 'Joe'?

'Make up your mind,' her tormentor ordered. 'We haven't got all day.'

With trembling fingers, Jo unzipped her anorak and started to lower her cargo pants. Then she got angry again and pulled the anorak off and flung it over the bonnet. She ripped her boots off and stepped out of her pants. 'You may look but don't you dare lay a finger on me again,' she ground out, her grey eyes flashing magnificently.

The man grimaced and raised his eyebrows. 'Well, well!' His gaze dwelt on her figure beneath a fitted, fine-knit blue jumper and pale blue cotton briefs, and drifted down her long legs.

'Just goes to show you shouldn't make snap judgements,' he said with humour, looking back into her eyes, 'since it would be fair to say that in other circumstances you'd be welcome to seduce me, love.' The humour left his eyes. 'Turn around.'

If she'd been angry before, Jo was boiling now, but caution had the upper hand. She turned and lifted her arms to shoulder height. 'Satisfied?' she asked over her shoulder.

'Yep.' She stiffened as she felt his fingers on her waist and the elastic of her briefs pinged against her skin. 'Good old Bonds Cottontails, I do believe,' he added. 'OK, get dressed, then we're going for a drive.'

Jo pulled on her cargo pants. 'A drive? How far?'

'Right into—' He paused. 'Why?'

She hesitated, unsure whether to confess that she'd somehow underestimated the distance to Kin Can homestead, and another of her concerns had been that she'd run out of petrol...

'Come on, Jo—' he unslung the gun menacingly '—talk!'

'I don't have much petrol left.'

He swore. 'Bloody women!'

'I believe there's a pump at the house so—'

'Told you that, did they? Well, it's not going to be of any use to me. Get in and switch on so I can see how low the tank is.'

Jo swallowed and finished dressing as quickly as she could. And when she switched the motor on and the petrol gauge was revealed—bordering the red— he swore again, even more murderously, then, 'No spare tanks?'

'No.'

'What are you? One of their molls press-ganged into providing back-up?'

'I have no idea what you're talking about!' Jo cried. 'None of this makes any sense.'

'Oh, yes, it does, sweetheart,' he replied insolently, then rubbed his jaw with a sudden tinge of weariness. It didn't last long, that first faint sign of weakness, however. 'Plan B, then,' he said grimly.

* * *

Ten minutes later, Jo was steering her vehicle over another diabolical track, but this time following her captor's directions.

She'd had no opportunity to escape, as he'd made it quite clear he would shoot her down if she made any attempt to run away. Her request to be told what was going on had received a 'don't act all innocent with me, lady' response.

And he'd quashed, with an impatient wave of his hand and virtually unheard, her solitary attempt to explain who she was, why she was on Kin Can station and her conviction that he was making a terrible mistake.

He'd also searched the vehicle before they'd set off, then glanced at her with a considering frown.

So she drove with a set mouth and her heart hammering; he wouldn't allow her to use the headlights and the light was almost gone.

'There,' he said, pointing to a darker shadow on the landscape. 'Pull into the shed on the other side.'

At first Jo thought it was only a clump of towering gum trees, then she discerned the outline of two buildings. 'What is it?'

'Boundary riders hut,' he replied tersely as she nosed the vehicle into an old shed.

'Is it…is this where you live?'

He laughed scornfully. 'Who are you trying to kid, Jo?'

She sucked in a breath. 'I'm not trying to kid anyone! I have no idea what's going on or who on earth you are! What's your name?'

He glanced at her mockingly. 'For the purpose of maintaining your charade, why don't you choose one? Tom, Dick or Harry will do.'

'I have a better idea,' she spat at him. 'Mr Hitler is particularly appropriate for what I think of you!'

'So the lady has claws,' he said softly, with an appreciative gleam in his blue eyes, and switched on the inside light.

'You better believe it.'

Their gazes clashed. It was an angry, defiant moment for Jo, but there was also fear lurking beneath it. Fear and something else—a certain amount of confusion. He might act like a bushranger or a boundary rider gone berserk, but he sounded like neither.

What he said was undoubtedly inflammatory and insulting—let alone the incomprehensibility of it all— but the voice was educated and cultured with the kind of accent that a wealthy, old-money family and a private school steeped in tradition would imbue.

Then there was his navy-blue jumper. If she was any judge, it would have cost a small fortune, being made of especially soft, fine new wool—although they were on a sheep station that specialized in fine new wool, weren't they?

But most perplexing of all was the frisson tiptoeing along her nerve ends in the form of an awareness of him stealing over her. If you discounted his stubbly jaw and his eyes that could be murderous, he was well proportioned, excellently co-ordinated and rather devastatingly good-looking...

'What?'

She blinked at his question. 'N-nothing.'

'Or—thinking of changing sides?' he suggested. 'Believe me, Jo, you'd be well advised to. Being my moll would have infinite advantages over—'

'Stop it!' She put her hands over her ears. 'I'm no one's *moll* and have no intention of becoming one!'

'No?' He said it consideringly with his gaze roaming over her narrowly. 'You could have fooled me a moment ago.'

Jo bit her lip and was furious with herself.

He laughed softly. 'You're not much good at this, are you?'

'If I had any idea what you're talking about—'

She broke off as he moved impatiently.

'Enough! Let's get inside. We'll take all your gear.'

'What for?'

'So I can go through it with a fine-tooth comb.' He clicked off the overhead light and jumped out.

She had no choice but to follow suit. The shed had doors and he pushed them closed and latched them, so unless you knew to look, there was no sign of her car. Then he gestured for her to precede him into the hut.

He did go through her things with a fine-tooth comb, but after he'd secured the hut and lit a fire in the rusty combustion stove from a store of chopped wood and old newspapers.

The wooden hut was small and rudimentary. It had a half-loft storing some bales of old straw, but the ladder to it was broken. There were a couple of uncomfortable-looking narrow beds, a table and two hard chairs, one dilapidated old armchair, a small store of dry and tinned goods and a couple of milk cans filled with water.

There was one high window, but it had been broken and boarded up, and one door. All the same, as a precaution against any light being seen, Jo gathered, he hung a blanket over the door and a rough, dingy towel over the window.

Two things he did she could only approve of: the light and warmth from the stove were welcome against the cold, dark night, and the aroma from the pot of coffee he set on the stove caused her to close her eyes in deep appreciation as she took her anorak off.

On the other hand, two things she noticed while they waited for the coffee added to her confusion. He looked at his wrist, as if to check his watch, then with a grimace of annoyance, pulled it from his pocket and laid it on the table. It had a broken band, she saw, but, although it was plain enough, it was also sleek, platinum and shouted very expensive craftsmanship.

A faint frown knitted her brow. A demented boundary rider with a couple-of-thousand-dollar watch? Then there were his jeans. Torn and dirty they might be, but they were also designer jeans if she was any judge.

'No milk, but there is sugar,' he said presently, and handed her an enamel mug. 'Help yourself.' He indicated a sugar caddy.

She took two spoonfuls and looked around as she stirred them in.

'Take the best chair, ma'am,' he said with some irony and indicated the armchair.

'Thanks,' she murmured and sank down into it. A small cloud of dust rose but she was too tired and tense to care and she realized she was still wearing her beanie. She plucked it off irritably, and turned to look at her captor as he made an involuntary sound.

She raised an eyebrow at him. 'What have I done now?'

'Er—nothing,' he responded. 'Why on earth do you cover your hair?'

Jo ran her fingers through her cloud of dark gold hair. Someone had once told her it was the colour of beech leaves in autumn. True or not, she regarded it as her crowning glory, perhaps her only glory, and it was certainly her only vanity, her long, thick, silky hair.

She pushed her fringe back and shrugged. 'It's cold and dusty out there.'

His blue gaze stayed on her in a rather unnerving manner and she felt a tinge of colour steal into her cheeks because she had no doubt he was contemplating her figure.

She would have died if she'd known that it had crossed his mind to wonder whether that deep rich gold colour of her hair was duplicated on her body...

He turned his attention rather abruptly to her two bags, unpacking the entire contents of the smaller one onto the table.

Jo sipped her coffee and watched as he went through every item of clothing she'd brought, her writing case, books, sponge bag and make-up, her first-aid kit. He upended her canvas tote bag and her diary, her phone, a map and her purse fell out together with a bag of sweets and some tissues.

He picked up the phone. 'This isn't any good to us out here, we're out of mobile range.'

'So I gathered,' she said bitterly.

He smiled unpleasantly. 'Did you try to get in touch with them after you left Cunnamulla? I would have thought they'd have warned you about that—or supplied you with a satellite phone. Joanne Lucas,' he read as he examined her credit card, her diary, her Medicare card and her driver's licence.

'If you go back to the diary, you'll find my address, my doctor, my dentist and possibly my plumber and electrician.' She eyed him ironically.

He didn't respond, but started to repack the bag. The sight of him handling her underwear again annoyed her intensely, however, and she jumped up. 'I'll do that!'

'OK.' He pushed it all down the table towards her and reached for the bigger bag. 'Painting gear, from the earlier look I took at it,' he said.

He took out a collapsible easel, a heavy box of oil crayons, charcoal pencils, a sheaf of cartridge paper and a smaller box of sharpeners and rubbers. 'Now that—' he sat back '—has to be an inspired bit of camouflage, Ms Lucas.'

'You can believe what you like but, as I tried to tell you earlier, I was commissioned by Mrs Adele Hastings of Kin Can station to do her portrait. That's why I'm here.'

'Mrs Adele Hastings is not on Kin Can.'

Jo stared at him. 'But I spoke to her only a few days ago to make the final arrangements!'

He shrugged and folded his arms.

'How do you know she's not there, anyway?' Jo asked.

'I…made it my business to know.'

Jo frowned. '*Are* you some demented, latter-day bushranger? Or a boundary rider gone berserk? Is that what this is all about?'

'Go on.'

'What do you mean, "go on"?' Her frustration was obvious. 'All I'm trying to do is make some sense of it.'

'Fascinating stuff,' he commented. 'Just say I were either of those, what would it lead you to assume?'

She gestured with both hands. 'You…held up the homestead, got sprung maybe, escaped, mistook me for reinforcements and took me hostage—' She broke off abruptly and her grey eyes dilated as she castigated herself for even mentioning the possibility.

He smiled. 'Well, it so happens I did escape, Jo. And not long before I did so, I heard them calling their back-up, by the name of Jo—Joe—whatever, and requesting confirmation of what the back-up vehicle would be. They repeated what they were told—a silver-grey Range Rover.'

This time her eyes virtually stood out on stalks. 'That's…that's—'

'Coincidence?' he suggested sweetly. 'I don't think so.' His mouth hardened. 'Then there's the fact that you drove in by the back gate, as instructed, which took you a long way out of your way but, being a woman, I presume, you neglected to think of the extra petrol you might need.'

Jo opened and closed her mouth a couple of times, then, 'So *that's* why it seemed a lot further than I'd calculated. But—' she stopped to think briefly '—what happened to the front gate?'

His gaze narrowed on her. 'You know,' he said at last, 'you might be whole lot cleverer than I first thought. You're certainly an inspired liar—what the hell could have happened to the front gate?'

Jo gritted her teeth. 'According to Mrs Adele Hastings, the front gate, the main gate, the *only* gate she mentioned should have been about fifty kilometres back from the gate I drove through. And it should have been well signposted. "You won't miss it," she told me. "It's a big black truck tyre with the name painted in white on it." Believe me, I kept my eyes peeled but I saw nothing like that.'

His eyes narrowed but he maintained the attack from a different direction. 'And you just kept on driving all those extra kilometres?' he taunted.

'Yes, I did! But only after I used my mobile phone to contact Kin Can only to find I'd gone out of range. That road was quite good, though, and I thought—what's fifty kilometres to country people?'

A glimmer of a smile lit his eyes but it was gone as soon as it came.

'Nevertheless, you have it right. I do intend to hold you hostage, sweetheart, so I hope you mean something to whoever you're working for, otherwise things could be a little nasty for you.' He stood up. 'Care for some soup? Or there's baked beans, uh, tinned spaghetti—'

Jo went to slap his face, only to end up pinned in his arms.

'Now, now, Lady Longlegs,' he said softly. 'You may be pretty athletic, but you're no match for me.'

'Don't call me that!'

'I'll call you what I like. I'm the man with the gun, remember?'

Jo shivered.

He felt it through her clothes and it crossed his mind again that, in different circumstances, Jo Lucas was his kind of woman—tall, with lovely, clean lines and some fascinating curves. As for her face, perhaps not a face to look twice at in the first instance, he thought, but once you did, it held the eye.

Her skin was smooth and creamy, but her lashes and eyebrows were darker than her hair and they framed her grey eyes admirably. Her nose was straight, her mouth was actually fascinating with a slightly swollen bee-stung upper lip that excited a rash impulse to kiss it he had to kill rather swiftly...

And the whole was completely natural, no trace of make-up, no plucking of her eyebrows into coy arches and, he glanced down at her hands, no painted nails.

So what does that all tell me? he wondered. She's a practical, serious-minded person but rather unexpectedly lovely in her own quiet way?

He chewed his lip and stilled the sudden movement she made to free herself and again their gazes clashed. He smiled inwardly at the proud expression in her grey eyes that told him she was hating every moment of being confined in his arms against her will.

If looks could kill, I should be six feet under, he reflected wryly. I wonder how she reacts to being made love to? Soberly or...

He paused his thoughts with an ironic lifting of his eyebrows, and she blinked in sudden confusion as if she'd been trying to read his mind, and failed.

Just as well, he mused with a certain humour, and attempted to direct his thoughts into a more businesslike channel, only to find himself speculating on how she'd got roped into this diabolical situation.

She was bound to be someone's lover, surely? Brought in on a tide of passion, perhaps—but no, it just didn't seem to fit her. Neither did she look venal, although it was hard to tell with women. But what was left? A grudge? What the hell could she, personally, have against him? A grudge against society, then, or...

That was when he paused to ask himself if there could be some mistake?

But how about all those coincidences? Too many to be believable? Yes. On the other hand, she appeared to have no suspicious equipment, no equipment at all other than a useless mobile phone. But did that preclude her from simply driving a back-up vehicle? It did not and he couldn't afford to take any chances anyway.

He let her go abruptly.

'I've had a thought,' she said quietly. 'While you're holding me hostage here, the real Joe, if there is such a person, is probably making his way to the homestead as we speak.'

His eyes narrowed again. 'Time will tell, lady.'

'Who are you?' It came out unwittingly and she bit her lip but, once said, she decided to persevere. 'At least tell me what's going on. Surely, as a hostage, I'm entitled to know what I've got myself into?'

Several expressions chased across his eyes—did she imagine it or was one of them a trace of perplexity? If so, it was immediately replaced with bland insolence.

'Got yourself into?' he repeated. 'A bed of your own making, I would imagine, Jo. In the meantime, I don't know about you, but it's going to be baked beans and biscuits for me.'

*   *   *

Two hours later, the hut was quiet and dim.

Jo had eaten a few spoonfuls of baked beans, she'd attended to a call of nature in the rough outhouse attached to the hut, and been attended in turn by her captor. When she'd finished, they'd both stood outside for a short time, listening and trying to probe the dense, chill darkness for any sign of life, but there had been none.

In Jo's case, she'd also been trying to get her bearings just in case an opportunity to escape came up.

Then he'd shepherded her inside and told her to go to sleep.

The beds were along the walls at right angles to each other, their thin grey and white ticking mattresses unadorned by sheets, although each bed had one dismal-looking pillow and one hairy-looking blanket.

She took her anorak off again and her boots, and prepared to lie down, but he stopped her suddenly.

'Get your night gear on,' he ordered.

'What for?'

'You are going to bed.'

She gestured contemptuously. 'You call this a bed?'

'It's all there is.'

'Perhaps, but I'd feel much happier in my clothes. There could be fleas, there could be ticks, there could be—anything.'

'All the same, Jo, I'd rather you got into your PJs. I'll get them for you.' He picked up her bag.

'No—hang on!' she protested with her hands planted on her hips. 'If you think I'm going to afford you some kind of a peep show, if that's why you want me to change into pyjamas, you're mistaken, Dick!'

He raised a lazy eyebrow and scanned her from head to toe. Her hands-on-hips posture and her straight back made the jut of her breasts particularly enticing beneath the fine pale blue wool of her jumper.

'What a pleasant thought,' he said softly, eyeing the outline of her nipples and the narrowness of her waist. 'But—' his lips twitched as she looked downwards and hastily amended her stance '—sadly, it wasn't what I had in mind. I fully intended to step outside while you changed.'

'So why…what…?' She stared at him in confusion.

'It's simple, sweetheart,' he said. 'You're much less likely to be running around the countryside in your nightwear, should you devise some devilish plan of escape. Apart from anything else—' he smiled at her with pure devilry '—you'd freeze. Don't be long,' he added. 'I'm not too happy about freezing either.' He stepped outside.

Jo unclenched her jaw and said every swear word she could think of beneath her breath. But there was nothing for it other than to retrieve the least revealing of the two pairs of pyjamas she'd packed, and change into them.

'Decent?' he called.

'*Yes.*'

'Decent and—mad,' he murmured as he came in, closed the door behind him and rearranged the blanket. 'Mmm.' He scanned her from head to toe. 'I see you kept your bra on. Not much protection against—anything, I would have thought.'

Jo looked down at her pyjamas. In a fine white cotton, with bands of filigree embroidery, her bra was visible beneath the top, but the alternative had been a pair of short, sleeveless pyjamas in a sensuous lilac satin.

She raised her gaze to his face. 'I'll get even with you one day for all this if it's the *last* thing I do.'

'Should be interesting. Go to bed, Jo.'

'What…what are you going to do?'

'Wait and watch, what else?'

'If you dare try crawling into my bed—' she began, but he cut her off.

'I don't actually hold with rape, whatever else you may think of me. I prefer my women warm and willing. Unless—' he cocked an eyebrow at her '—a bit of hostility is what turns you on?'

'You're disgusting,' she said through her teeth.

He laughed softly. 'There is quite—a body of evidence that would disagree with you.'

'I can imagine. Gangster molls, no doubt.'

His expression cooled. 'Certainly none of them have been as good an actress as you are, my dear.' He turned away to pick up her boots, her anorak and her bag of clothes and he slung them onto the loft.

Jo could have screamed from frustration. Instead, with an expression of rigid distaste but supreme self-control, she lay down on the bed and pulled the blanket up.

Sleep, of course, was the furthest thing from her mind, although she closed her eyes a couple of times as the fire in the stove burnt low, and her captor lounged back in the armchair—with his gun across his knees.

If she could feign sleep, she reasoned, perhaps he would lower his guard, even fall asleep himself? But what could she do if she managed to sneak out of the hut? He had her car keys in his pocket and he'd locked the car; her clothes and boots were out of reach. And, as he had so diabolically foreseen, running around the rough terrain outside in her bare feet and pyjamas was highly unappealing if not to say inviting pneumonia and injury.

But perhaps I could hide, she mused. He doesn't appear to have a torch and perhaps I could sneak a blanket out with me?

She strained her eyes in the gloom and stared at the door. There was no lock, only a bolt on the inside and—her heart started to beat faster as she remembered—a bolt on the outside as well. How much better if she could not only sneak out and find a place to hide, but lock the man inside the hut as well? If he was trying to escape detection for whatever reason, he'd hardly shoot his way out of the hut...

She took some deep breaths to compose herself and moved slightly. The bed squeaked a bit but he didn't stir.

Gotcha, she thought, but decided to wait a while longer in case he was only cat-napping.

Ten minutes later, she sat up cautiously, and waited. No movement from the armchair, so she eased herself off the bed and flinched at the series of squeaks. Still no movement from the chair, though, but she stood quietly, trying to adjust her eyes to the gloom. The fire was nearly out in the stove but eventually she could see him. He was sprawled out with his head back and one arm hanging over the side of the chair.

The gun was still in his lap and an almost overwhelming temptation came to her—she only had to steal forward and grab it—but she had no knowledge of guns at all. What was there to know, though? Anyone could pull a trigger, not necessarily *at* him, but if he knew she was prepared to fire the damn gun wouldn't that be enough?

Then he moved and she froze. But all he did was turn slightly and bring his arm up so that his hand rested across the gun. And he muttered something unintelligible, but slept on.

Almost weak with relief, Jo stayed where she was for a few minutes, but decided that grabbing the gun was out—she could get herself shot. And she lifted the blanket off the bed and tiptoed towards the door where, with infinite care, she moved the blanket covering it aside and eased the bolt ever so slowly backwards.

'Nice try, darling.'

She nearly jumped a foot off the floor and lurched round to find him standing behind her with the gun pointed straight at her heart. How he'd got there so soundlessly was a mystery.

'Wh-what woke you?' she stammered.

'Don't know. Some sixth sense, maybe. What—' he looked at her ironically '—did you hope to achieve, Jo?'

Her shoulders slumped. 'I don't know. But,' she said with more spirit, 'I couldn't just lie there and accept—fate or whatever!'

He stared down at her. There was an agitated pulse thudding at the base of her throat and her eyes were wide and terrified but also stubborn.

He heaved an inward sigh and lowered the gun. Whatever she was, this woman was getting to him, he acknowledged. There were things he couldn't help admiring about her. You had to be brave to try to escape out into an unknown landscape on a frigid night with no shoes and only an old blanket.

But he still couldn't afford to take the chance that she wasn't who she said she was, however brave and—all the rest.

He turned away to put some more wood in the stove, then he stretched and studied his options. He had no idea what had woken him but one thing he did know—over twenty-four hours without sleep was taking its toll and his gaze fell longingly on the beds.

'OK,' he said, 'here's what we'll do.' He pushed her bed lengthwise against the other one, closing it in against the wall. 'You hop into that one—' he indicated the one against the wall '—and I'll use this one.'

She opened her mouth to protest but he forestalled her wearily. 'Jo, you're in no physical danger from me. However, I should warn you that the only way you can escape from that bed is to climb over me, and you mightn't find me in as conciliatory a mood were you to try. Now will you hop in?'

She hesitated, then did as she was told, to lie with her back to the second bed. He put her blanket over her and lay down, grappling with his own.

He was right, she realized. There was probably two inches' leeway from the other walls at the head and the foot of both beds so she was effectively penned in. She sighed and wriggled a bit to get comfortable.

A sleepy voice behind her said, 'You're right. These are only an apology for beds. You'll be pleased to hear, if you are Joanne Lucas, wandering portrait painter, that the beds up at the homestead are much more comfortable.'

'How would you know?'

'I've tried 'em.'

Jo frowned. 'These people you imagine I'm part of—who are they? And why are you running from them?'

'Kidnappers, as if you didn't know.'

Jo cast her blanket aside and sat up. 'Oh, this is ridiculous! Why would anyone, but particularly me, want to kidnap you?'

'For my sins,' her captor said, 'I happen to be Gavin Hastings the Fourth.'

CHAPTER TWO

JO WAS struck speechless for several minutes, but her mind was jumping as she recalled her several conversations with Mrs Adele Hastings, his—if he was who he said he was—mother!

She could only describe Adele Hastings as talkative. A child called Rosie had featured frequently in her conversations, but Jo had never been able to work out whose child she was.

Her son Gavin had also featured prominently, so that Jo was in the possession, quite ancillary to the business of doing the lady's portrait, of a store of knowledge about Gavin Hastings.

He was an excellent son, a bit high-handed at times, mind you, a bit prone to getting his own way, but extremely capable, he could turn his hand to just about anything, which he needed to be able to do to run the vast Hastings empire inherited from his father...and so Mrs Hastings had gone on, although admittedly in very well-bred tones.

Jo had done a bit of research on the family and discovered that it *was* quite a dynasty. The first Gavin Hastings had been a pioneer. His grandson, Gavin's father, had not only extended the family holdings, he'd diversified into cattle. He'd also married Adele Delaney, daughter of a press baron. Jo hadn't researched any further since it was Adele's portrait she was doing.

How come, though, she wondered, Adele hadn't told her excellent, high-handed—that bit was quite believable!—son about the portrait? And how come Mrs Hastings wasn't on Kin Can? On the other hand, if he was who he said he was, it explained the fine clothes, the watch, the cultured accent, although it still seemed incomprehensible he didn't know about the portrait.

She looked down at her captor to pose this question to him, but Gavin Hastings the Fourth was fast asleep.

Jo sank back to her pillow thoughtfully. The light from the stove was stronger now and she didn't have to peer through the gloom to make out his features. In repose, he looked younger, but she guessed he was around thirty-four.

Sleep, however, didn't diminish his good looks, although it did present him as much less arrogant. Above the bristles his skin was lightly tanned, his dark eyebrows less satanic, and his mouth that could be so hard or smile so sardonically, insolently, ironically—she had a whole range of less-than-pleasant expressions to recall even after such a short acquaintance—was relaxed and well cut.

One couldn't doubt, she decided, that, all spruced up, Gavin Hastings would be dynamically attractive.

He could also be extremely unpleasant, she reminded herself. He could be cutting and unforgivably personal even if he was being pursued by a gang of kidnappers—and she still had to prove to him she was no 'gangster's moll'.

Perhaps if she drew his portrait he'd believe her? Not now, of course, but at the first opportunity. As for being in a kidnap situation with him...

Her tired brain gave up at that point, and she fell asleep.

She had no idea how much later it was when she was wrenched awake by a drumming sound. She sat up with her hand to her throat and a dry mouth, only to feel someone's arm slide around her and hear a voice say, 'It's rain. Good news, really.'

'Who…what…?' It all came tumbling back to her. '*Rain!* It sounds like a machine gun!'

'Old tin roof, no insulation, that's all.'

Jo shivered. There was no sign of light coming from the stove and it was very cold. 'Why good news?' she asked.

'Should make it harder for them to find us, assuming they're still looking—I don't know about you, but I'm freezing.'

'You could always build up the fire,' she suggested.

She heard a low chuckle. 'Got a better idea. Lie back, Miss Lucas—I presume it is Miss?'

Jo ignored the question and asked one of her own. 'Why?'

'So we can cuddle up and put both blankets over us.'

'That is not on my agenda!'

'Well, it is on mine.' And Jo found herself being propelled backwards into his arms.

'I always suspected it would come to this,' she said bitterly.

'What?'

She swallowed.

'You have a bad mind, Josie,' he said into her hair. 'Are you off men for some reason? Is that why there's this intense suspicion?'

'Sharing a bed with a stranger—being forced to,' she amended, 'is enough to make any woman suspicious, surely? Not to mention all the rest of it. After all, you were the one who brought up seduction in the first place.'

'For my sins again,' he murmured. 'But you have to admit it's warmer like this.'

It was. It also felt—she couldn't quite work out why—safer. Because she knew who he was now? And knew she was on the side of the 'goodies'? Still very much suspect, of course, she reminded herself, but talk about a series of incredible coincidences!

One thing she was certain of, though, she had not missed Kin Can's main gate, so what *had* happened to it?

She opened her mouth, not only to bring that up, but so much more. Did he have any idea who his potential kidnappers were? How had he escaped them? But his deep, slow breathing and the relaxation of his arm about her waist told her he was asleep again.

She smiled unexpectedly. So much for seduction. But if you could believe what he himself had alluded to, a body of evidence—a whole lot of women who found him attractive, in other words—suggested he was a much safer bet asleep.

What kind of women appealed to *him*? she wondered suddenly. Gorgeous? Definitely. Sexy? Had to be. Joanne Lucas?

She moved abruptly and removed herself from beneath his arm and slid cautiously onto the other bed, still trying to share both blankets. He didn't move at all.

*   *   *

It was barely dawn when Gavin Hastings stirred and lay still again. Then he sniffed and frowned. His cheek was resting against someone's hair, hair that felt silky soft and gave up the faint fragrance of—what?

For some reason, a bottle of shampoo swam into his mental vision, a clear plastic bottle decorated with apples and pears and filled with green liquid—of course! Amongst Joanne Lucas's toiletries had been just such a bottle of shampoo; it was her hair and it smelled very faintly of pears.

Something else from her toiletries swam into his mind; a pink lady's razor with which, no doubt, she shaved those long, lovely legs. He rubbed his jaw wistfully. Even a pink razor would be extremely welcome to someone who hadn't shaved for two days.

Then his mind wandered onto another pleasure—the woman sleeping peacefully in his arms. Her body was soft and warm against his, in fact her curves felt sensational nestled into him and, he reflected ruefully, he had better get himself out of this situation before a certain claim he'd made earlier proved to be incorrect.

But, as he moved Jo Lucas gently away from him, she murmured softly, a small sound of protest, and she buried her head against his shoulder.

A spark of humour lit his eyes. You're going to hate me when I make mention of this, Josie, and if you get on your high horse again, as you most likely will, I shall no doubt bring it up...won't be able to resist it!

The humour died as he stared down at the sleeping

girl in his arms. Not only the perfume of her hair, but her smooth, soft skin and her warm, lovely body teased his senses.

His memory took flight again, not to a bottle of shampoo this time, but the vision of her without her cargo pants and the high, rounded swell of her hips beneath a pair of no-nonsense Bonds Cottontails. If she was a pleasure to study from the front, he thought, it would surely be a sheer pleasure to watch her walking away from you with those hips swinging beneath a flimsy skirt...

He dragged his mind back with an effort. Who the hell was she? Not only that, how often had he used women to make him forget, only to find they were an anodyne but not the real thing?

He got out of the bed less than gently and stretched vigorously. When he turned back, Jo's eyes were open, and completely bewildered.

'Morning, Miss Lucas,' he said briskly. 'Time to get back to the fray.'

Jo stayed exactly as she was for a long moment, then she sat up abruptly and combed her hair back with her fingers. 'Good morning.'

'Sleep well?' he enquired with a mocking tinge of irony.

'I...er...must have. I don't seem to remember much about it.'

'Just as well.' He waited, bastard that he was, as her eyes looked confused again, then he changed the subject completely. 'You may not have noticed but it's still raining. Here's what I suggest—we make use of your fold-up umbrella to visit the outhouse, then you can do what you like while I do a recce.'

'Do what I like?' Jo repeated uncertainly.

'Get dressed in peace, perhaps heat some water on the stove for a wash—I'll build up the fire—or, contemplate your navel if that's what you prefer to do at this hour of the morning.'

Her eyes darkened and he knew it would have given her great pleasure to tell him to get lost, but in much more colourful language. She kept her mouth shut, however, and climbed out of bed.

'Here.' Something made him take pity on her, and he reached for her anorak. 'Wear this.'

She accepted it but refused to look at him, even when he pulled her bags and boots down as well.

Fifteen minutes later Jo was on her own in the hut, bolted in from the outside to her intense annoyance, but he had got the fire going and there were both the coffee-pot and a pot of water for washing simmering on the stove.

After a brief wash and dressing in a fleecy-lined grey tracksuit, she felt a lot better. She brushed her hair and tied it back and made herself a pot of coffee. And she pictured Gavin Hastings reconnoitring with, not only her fold-up umbrella, but the plastic poncho she always carried—neither of which would afford him great protection, but they had to be better than nothing in the downpour outside.

Gavin Hastings, she reflected, who had made a nasty little remark about something it was just as well she couldn't remember—*what*?

She surely couldn't have slept through his taking advantage of her in any way. She surely wouldn't have taken advantage of *him* in any way so...?

She glanced over at the two beds. Only one of them, narrow as it was, still bore the sagging imprint of being slept on. She clicked her teeth together in sheer annoyance.

She must have spent the night in his arms, right up close and personal. Only two bodies in one dilapidated old bed made for one body would cause it to stay sagged like that. To make it worse, the sagging bed was his, the bed on the outside, so she must have been the one to move over.

Clearly a tactical error, she thought, even if I was half asleep. I must have been cold and *scared*—I must have been mad!

The coffee-pot bubbled at that point, so she poured herself a mug and tried to turn her mind away from things she couldn't change. Then she remembered her idea of doing his portrait in a bid to prove she was who she'd said she was.

It turned out to be an exercise with curious side effects as she opened her pencil box and tore a piece of cartridge paper in half...

She'd always been a sketcher. For as long as she could remember, she'd doodled and etched and found it a great comfort, but paints had never particularly appealed to her. She'd tried watercolours, oils and acrylics but found that none of them was her medium.

At eighteen, however, her life had changed dramatically and she'd gone to art school for a year. That was where she'd discovered oil crayons—and it had all fallen into place. It had not been a lack of colour appreciation, her failure with paint, it had been her difficulty in merging the two techniques, drawing and painting.

Oil crayons allowed her to draw in colour, and she virtually hadn't stopped since the discovery. So that now, at twenty-four, she had a small but growing reputation in portraiture.

Of course, doing portraits had its downside. You were often at the mercy of less-than-likeable characters and your fingers itched to portray them that way. It had, however, gained her recognition, and once that reputation was well established she would be able to draw what she pleased and sell it—landscapes and particularly children, whom she loved to draw, although not necessarily as their parents wanted them portrayed.

As she organized herself as best she could, she practised a familiar technique. She breathed deeply and cleared her mind—and she called up her captor.

As always, some emotions came with the image she was seeing in her mind's eye, her reaction to her subject, but what caused her to blink in surprise was the veritable kaleidoscope of emotions that came along with Gavin Hastings's dark, good-looking face.

She discovered that her fingers longed to score and slash lines and angles onto the paper with her crayons in a caricature of the devil with very blue eyes.

Jo, Jo, she chided herself, if he's to be believed, he's been subject to a kidnap attempt so he's bound to be antsy!

Doesn't matter, she retorted. I don't like him, but I especially don't like the way I *do* like some things about this man I don't like. And I resent wondering, actually wondering, what he thinks of me!

She stared down at the still-pristine piece of paper beneath her fingers and was horrified to find herself breathing raggedly. This isn't going to work, she thought. There's only one way I can draw Gavin Hastings with any peace of mind and that's asleep.

She had no idea how much later it was when she heard the bolt being withdrawn on the other side of the door, but some instinct made her throw her anorak over all the evidence of her endeavours.

He came in looking as mean and nasty as any demented bushranger, daubed with mud and soaking wet.

Her eyes widened, then she looked at her watch and realized he'd been away for over an hour. 'Are you all right?' she asked.

'Concerned for me, maybe even missed me?' he queried sardonically. 'No, I'm not all right. Put some water on to boil.'

Jo opened her mouth to take issue with his manner, then changed her mind, and he started to peel off his clothes.

'Uh—what happened to the umbrella and the poncho?' she ventured.

'They were about as useless as a pocket handkerchief so I threw them away.'

Joanne listened to the rain pounding on the roof for a moment. 'Yes, well, they weren't designed for this kind of downpour.' She refilled the coffee-pot and set it on the stove. 'Did you—achieve anything?' She turned to look at him, but turned away abruptly—he was down to his underpants and socks. Then she took hold and told herself not to be spinsterish. 'Here.'

She took a blanket off the bed and handed it over. He didn't thank her as he draped it around him.

Instead, as their gazes met his was full of such chilling scorn that she flinched.

She had to say, 'Look, none of this is my fault. It's no good being angry with me. If anything, it's counterproductive.'

'Really.' He sat down at the table. 'Have you been able to come up with anything *pro*ductive while you've been twiddling your thumbs?' he asked unpleasantly.

She set her teeth.

'Well, I'll tell you what I've been doing,' he said. 'Skulking around my own property, stealing my own fuel, which I then had to carry like a packhorse, while you've been—' his gaze strayed to a corner of the pencil box protruding from beneath her anorak and he swept the jacket aside '—I don't believe this— painting!'

'It's not painting. I don't use paints. I use oil crayons.'

'Nevertheless—' He stopped and studied his portrait, but what he thought of it she was destined not to know because, although he blinked once, he then looked up at her with palpable menace. 'Do you honestly think this proves anything?'

'I...' She bit her lip. 'I was hoping it would.'

'Then you thought wrong, lady. So—' he relaxed somewhat, but the attack didn't relax at all as he studied the portrait again '—you looked your fill while I was asleep, Jo?'

Some colour came to her cheeks. 'It's a habit I have. Bones, lines, angles, muscles are my stock-in-trade.'

'What about cuddling up to strange men?'

The hiss of droplets turning to steam on the stove top told her the water had boiled, but she ignored it. 'I must have been asleep. I certainly don't remember doing it. I must have been cold—that's all there is to it.'

He watched her set mouth and returned her level grey gaze for a moment, then shrugged. 'It was very pleasant, as it happens. Would you be so kind as to clear the table, Miss Lucas, and would you lend me your pink razor?'

Jo parted her lips, but then closed them.

'You're right,' he said as if she'd spoken, 'I need a shave. It might even put me in a better frame of mind. You wouldn't happen to have a mirror?'

She had more. She had a small cake of soap, a clean, slightly damp towel, a toothbrush and toothpaste, but the mirror was tiny.

He used it all the same, squinting at it humorously for any patches of bristle he'd missed. Then he cleaned his teeth with heartfelt relief.

'I like a lady with a good, sharp razor,' he commented at one stage. 'New?' He held it up to the light.

'It was new,' Jo agreed dryly.

He laughed. 'Might not be good for much after ploughing through that beard, but if we ever get out of here, Jo, I'll buy you another one. Ouch.' He fingered his jaw. 'You wouldn't have any aftershave lotion, by any chance?'

'If that's designed to make me feel less than feminine,' she said pointedly, 'it's like water off a duck's back. No, I don't, but you could try this.' She handed him a bottle out of her toilet bag.

He turned it over in his hands and read the label. 'Witch hazel? What's that?'

'A very good, natural astringent that should make your skin feel all tingly and fresh.'

'Ah.' He poured some into his palms and slapped it on his face. 'You're right! A woman of great resource. Incidentally—' he screwed the cap on the bottle '—I thought I'd dispelled that less-than-feminine tag?'

During his ministrations, he'd shoved the blanket down to his waist and she had picked up his wet clothes and hung them on the other chair in front of the fire.

'I don't give a damn about what you think of me in that regard,' she replied, but the truth was the sleek muscles of his shoulders, the springy dark hair on his chest, his tapering, rock-hard torso were all hard to ignore for two reasons. The funny little sensation they brought to the pit of her stomach and a very real desire to capture such male perfection on paper.

There was a little silence. Then he said ironically, 'You're a hard nut to crack, Josie.'

She shrugged and busied herself with making breakfast—this time tinned stew and biscuits. But her fingers stilled as she remembered what he'd said earlier, and she turned to him suddenly. 'Fuel?'

His eyes narrowed. 'I wondered when that would sink in,' he murmured.

'So you got some? How? Did you get up to the house?'

He shook his head. 'There's a machinery shed not that far away.'

She turned back to the stew. 'So we're...we can...go?'

'No. There's a creek up and running between us and the gate we wouldn't get through even in a four-wheel drive at the moment.'

Jo served up breakfast. She handed him a knife and fork, then sat in the armchair with her plate balanced on her knees and chose her next words with care.

'There are some things I don't understand. Were you completely alone on the station when they kidnapped you?'

'No, I wasn't. The head stockman was—immobilized before they came after me.'

'Not killed?' Her eyes were dark with shock.

'No. But captured and tied up and removed heaven alone knows where.' He started to eat with evident hunger.

'And there was no family, no one else?' she asked with a frown.

'Jo—' he paused with his fork poised and glinted her an assessing look '—whoever they are, they'd done their homework. It's a long weekend, it happens to be the district's annual rodeo with all its attendant parties, B and S balls and the like. A lot of people are away from home, in other words. It so happens *I* was supposed to be away from home but I changed my mind at the last minute.'

'Is that why your mother isn't home?' she asked perplexedly.

This time he waved his fork. 'My mother took off for Brisbane two days ago. Some show she'd forgotten she had tickets for. I can only be grateful she wasn't there and neither, particularly, was Rosie.'

Suddenly, his blue gaze seemed to drill right through her.

Jo blinked. 'She mentioned a Rosie several times when we spoke on the phone—a child, I gathered, but I couldn't work out whose.'

He stared at her for another long moment, then finished his breakfast and put his knife and fork together. 'Mine.'

Jo digested this with several blinks. 'Well, what about your wife?' she ventured.

'She died in childbirth.' He pushed his plate away and there was something completely dark and shuttered in his expression. 'Any chance of a cup of coffee?'

'Of course,' Jo murmured and got up to attend to it. 'Would...' she hesitated '...would I be right in assuming your mother is a tad absent-minded?'

He looked heavenwards. 'My mother, God bless her, has developed a memory like a sieve lately.'

'Well—' Jo put a mug of coffee in front of him '—that explains it!'

'You mean it explains why she forgot you were due to descend on Kin Can?'

'Yes!' Jo put her hands on her hips.

'Doesn't explain why she never once mentioned anything about getting her portrait painted—drawn, whatever—to me.'

Jo subsided. 'Perhaps she meant to surprise you?'

'So how do you think she was going to explain you, in the flesh, away?'

'I don't know—she's *your* mother!'

'For my sins—yet again,' he said dryly, and got up. 'I don't suppose you have any men's clothing in your bag of tricks?' he added moodily and hitched the blanket around him again.

Jo merely stared at him steadily.

'Once again, if looks could kill I'd be six feet under. OK, Miss Lucas, assuming you are lily-white, above board and all the rest, do you have any suggestions?'

Jo resisted the urge to give vent to her feelings—she posed a question instead. 'How many are there?'

'Two. They wore balaclavas so I have no idea who they are.'

'How did you escape?'

He sat down on the corner of the table. 'Checking up on me, Jo?'

'I do only have your word for it.'

He mulled over this for a moment, then grimaced. 'They trussed me up like a chicken and locked me overnight in a windowless storeroom. What they didn't know was that under the lino there was a trap-door—the house is on stilts about two feet above the ground, handy in times of flood. I got away through it.'

'How? If you were trussed up like a chicken?'

He rubbed his wrists and Jo noticed, for the first time, almost red-raw, chafing marks on the inside of each wrist. 'I found a pair of old scissors and managed to saw through the rope with them. Not that easy since my hands were tied against my back.'

'No,' she agreed with a tinge of awe, which she immediately tried to mask by adding, 'Why didn't they take you away instead of storing you in the house for a whole night?'

He glanced at her. 'Well, you see, Josie, I wasn't their target.'

She stared at him blankly.

'No,' he said meditatively and rubbed his chin. 'It was Rosie they'd planned to snatch, my six-year-old daughter—a much softer target.'

Jo's mouth fell open.

'As you say.'

'But...are you sure?'

'I'm quite sure. I heard all the discussion, all the recriminations going on throughout the night, all the new plans being made. They decided since they'd got me they'd take me in her place, but that's why they called for some back-up.'

'Thank heavens for your mother's bad memory,' Jo said a little shakenly.

'All the same, not only do I have to get myself off Kin Can, I have to prevent my mother and Rosie waltzing back into their arms. They cut all the phone lines, you see.'

'Won't that make people—your mother—suspicious?'

'Not necessarily. The system can have its problems out here and it is rodeo weekend.'

'I do have a suggestion,' she said slowly. 'Not to do with how to escape, but I feel pretty sure they must have also removed...any indication it was Kin Can station from the main gate. Perhaps to confuse anyone looking for the place?'

He gave it some thought as well as tossing her a considering look.

'Believe me,' she said quietly, 'that is why you found me on the back track.'

'Hmm… You could be right.' He shrugged. 'The main problem now is—have they given up and gone away? Or, are they waiting to trap me somehow, even out searching for me?'

'They don't sound terribly well organized.'

He stood up, cast the blanket off and reached for his clothes. 'Fate may have conspired against them, the weather certainly has, but they're a dangerous duo—trio if Joe got through. One of them, at least, is using a mixture of drugs and alcohol to keep himself hepped up.'

Jo shivered and watched as he struggled into his damp jeans, T-shirt and jumper. 'Did they offer you any violence? Other than tying you up?'

His lips twisted. 'A kick in the kidneys, a wallop over the head—' he searched his scalp through his dark hair and winced as he obviously found a bump '—and several others, but perhaps I gave them some provocation.'

'You didn't go quietly?' she hazarded.

'No, my dear, I didn't.'

Something in the way he said it chilled Jo to the core. She had no doubt Gavin Hastings would be a bad man to cross.

'As for the rest of it, they had the foresight to im-mobilize every other vehicle up at the house and they locked the dogs in the shed and threw away the key. The gun was a lucky break for me. Case, the foreman, must have forgotten to put it away in the gun cup-board in the shed. I nearly tripped over it.'

Jo collected the tin plates and empty mugs and stacked them on the floor next to the stove. 'So your plan was to intercept the other Joe and...?' She looked a question at him.

'Force him to drive me to the nearest phone.' He watched her as she swept some biscuit crumbs off the table with her hand, and she became aware that the lurking suspicion was back in his eyes.

'Silver-grey Range Rovers are pretty common, you know.'

'Perhaps. How about a Joe and a Jo?'

She hesitated. 'I—'

But a crack of sound split the air and a bullet tore through one wall and buried itself in the opposite wall.

For a second they both froze, then Gavin Hastings leapt off the table and in a flying rugby tackle crashed her to the floor only just before another shot splintered the door around the bolt. Two minutes later the door had been kicked open and a man with a gun and wearing a balaclava was standing over them.

'Well, lookee here, Joe,' he snarled over his shoulder. 'Gav's got himself a girl. Pretty kinky keeping your mistress stashed away in an old boundary riders' hut, don't you reckon, guys?'

CHAPTER THREE

THE next few hours were the stuff of nightmares.

Jo and Gavin Hastings were tied up and loaded into a van. The second vehicle they were using was almost identical to Jo's Range Rover. But the crudity of the humour levelled at Jo was appalling and she was in no mood to appreciate that she was completely vindicated in Gavin Hastings's eyes. She was far too scared to even glance him an I-told-you-so look.

Nor could she do anything other than blink a couple of times when the kidnappers retrieved Gavin's gun, only to cast it aside in disgust when it was revealed to have no bullets.

Then the humour turned sour when the realization hit the kidnappers that the creek between them and the back gate was not negotiable. A heated argument ensued until it was finally decided they'd have to return to the homestead and take the track from it to the main gate.

But that didn't work for them either. The van got bogged about a quarter of a mile from the house. She and Gavin had their feet untied and were frogmarched up a winding, tree-lined driveway by two of the kidnappers, while the third, using the Range Rover, attempted to tow it out of the mud.

Her first impressions of Kin Can homestead, therefore, were blurred by rain and fear. All she could say was that it looked vast.

And as they reached the front steps a nasty little fracas developed as one of the men put his arms around her and tried to kiss her. Gavin swung his arms tied at the wrist and clouted the man on the head. He went down like a ninepin, but then so did Gavin Hastings as he was punched in the face by the other one.

Finally, they were manhandled up the front steps and into the house. Again her impressions were over-laid by fear, but she couldn't help the startled thought that the house was a work of art, spacious, beautifully furnished and the essence of luxury.

After more argument they were locked into a bed-room. As an added precaution, one of the kidnappers untied the cords around their wrists, but produced a pair of handcuffs and manacled Jo and Gavin to-gether. 'Try sawing that off,' he jeered.

It was a while before Jo caught her breath. They'd collapsed onto the bed after being shoved into the room. But she sat up eventually, and wondered if her companion had blacked out—there was no movement from Gavin Hastings.

'Are you OK?' she asked anxiously and lifted her hand. His came up with it. 'This is ridiculous!' She studied their linked hands joined by the shiny silver cuffs.

'Mmm...' he agreed. 'Right out of a very bad gangster movie.' And with an effort, he heaved him-self into a sitting position. 'But before I say any more, may I offer you my apologies, Miss Lucas?'

Jo opened her mouth, then closed it with the faintest smile curving her lips.

'That's being very generous, Jo,' he said gravely.

'I would have forgiven you for calling me all the unprintable names under the sun.'

'Oh, I haven't had time to work out if I've forgiven you or not.'

One eyebrow shot up. 'So why the smile—it looked like forgiveness.'

'It may have looked like it but I was actually thinking that all shaved and cleaned up you were rather—pretty. That is no longer the case.'

'*Pretty!*' He looked genuinely horrified.

'Well, good-looking, then,' she amended.

'What's wrong with me now?'

She shook her head sorrowfully. 'You have all the makings of a magnificent black eye, but I do thank you for springing to my defence the way you did.'

'So I should think,' he retorted, and with his free hand gingerly explored the swollen area around his eye, and he swore freely.

'What are we going to do?' she asked quietly.

'I had a thought—' he ground his teeth '—but the bastards are getting more dangerous by the minute. I get the feeling there's an element of panic beneath the gung-ho attitude—what do you reckon?'

She could only agree but added, 'I did think one of them, the tallest guy, seemed a little less.. gung-ho, though. Maybe he'd listen to some sense?'

'Such as?'

Jo shrugged. 'You could point out that you have no idea who they are and their best bet would be to shake the mud of Kin Can off their boots as fast as possible rather than kidnapping *anyone*—let alone two people.'

'Not just a pretty face,' he commented. 'My own

sentiments entirely. I even thought of offering to help them on their way, monetarily, although that goes supremely against the grain. But now you're involved—' He broke off at the sound of raised voices. 'The thieves have fallen out, by the sound of it.'

Jo shivered.

'Can't put my arm around you,' he said humorously, 'but consider it done mentally.'

She smiled ruefully.

'That's better. OK, let's attract their attention and attempt to parley. One, two, stand up!'

Jo stood up with him and moved alongside him to the door. He rapped loudly on it. It was opened after a while by the tall man Jo had taken for being the less gung-ho of the three.

Ten minutes later it closed on them and was locked from the outside.

'Think he bought it?' Gavin enquired. The tallest of the three kidnappers had gone away with the expressed intention of consulting his 'colleagues'.

'I don't know. Only time will tell, I guess.' Her shoulders slumped.

He looked down at her critically. 'In the meantime—and I think you've been wonderful, Jo, most women I know would have had hysterics at least by now—we might as well make ourselves comfortable.' He indicated the bed.

Jo looked down at the soggy mess they both were. 'We'll make a mess.'

He grimaced. 'Who cares? Now, the key to it is for us both to sit down on it and gradually manoeuvre ourselves into a supine position—boots off, naturally.'

Several awkward moments later they were lying side by side on the bed, propped up by some wonderfully full, soft pillows.

'I see what you mean about a superior standard of bedding in the homestead,' she remarked, and looked around the room.

He grinned. 'My mother has very superior ideas when it comes to, not only interior design, but clothes, cars, the lot.'

Jo could only agree with the interior design bit. Although it wasn't large, and most probably a spare bedroom, the décor was lovely and no expense had been spared. A crisp cream waffle bedspread, although not so clean any longer, fuchsia-pink walls, cream woodwork and a tall, gorgeous dresser, cream again with brass handles. There were flower prints on the walls and Roman blinds at the window. There were also security insect screens over the window, fastened from the outside.

'No trapdoor under the carpet?' she asked.

'No, sadly. And no likelihood of any helpful implements in the drawers or cupboard.'

'There could be, surely?'

He shook his head. 'The room was cleaned out completely prior to being redecorated recently.'

'Oh.'

He turned to study her profile. 'I'm sorry I got you into this.'

'I probably would have got into it anyway, bad timing sort of thing.' She flinched and stiffened as the level of voices rose outside the door.

He listened for a while, then took her hand, the one manacled to his. 'Tell me about yourself, Jo Lucas.'

'I...' She made an effort to tear her mind away from the kidnappers. 'I...well, I'm an orphan. My parents died in a train crash when I was six and I went to live with my maternal grandmother. I was twelve when she developed Alzheimer's Disease so I was transferred to a series of foster homes. She died when I was fifteen.'

His hand tightened on hers.

She gestured with her free hand. 'There was a happy ending—of sorts. My father had been estranged from his family, well, his father, and they'd completely lost track of each other. He was English and he'd originally emigrated to Canada but came on to Australia.' She paused.

'Is this painful?' he queried.

'Uh—it's more like water under the bridge,' she said slowly. 'His mother had never stopped trying to find him, though, and she kept him, or his immediate descendants, in her will. When she died it took her lawyers another six years to track me down but they finally did when I was eighteen. So I came into a bit of money and I was able to put myself through art school and support myself ever since.'

'You'd be middle-twenties now?' he hazarded.

'Yep—twenty-four.'

'So how's it been otherwise since you were eighteen?'

'Fine.'

'I meant emotionally, relationships and the like. Sounds like a pretty traumatic upbringing to me.'

'It had its ups and downs,' she conceded.

'And it left no marks?'

Jo hesitated, then swallowed as a loud crash was

heard, and perhaps because of the horror and danger of the situation, she found herself telling him more than she'd told anyone for a long time.

'Ah, I have a slight problem there. Can't seem to bring myself to rely on anyone else. Not that it's a real problem. I mean, I'm perfectly happy as I am.'

'A loner,' he said after a long moment.

'A loner who loves it.'

'But you do have friends?'

'Of course. I went to school with my flatmate, Leanne Thomson. I keep in touch regularly with two of my foster families, as well as one of my art teachers, and so on.'

'What about men?'

Jo opened her mouth, then closed it and stared at the ceiling briefly. Surely there were some things you couldn't tell a perfect stranger even in these circumstances?

'I'm not good with men,' she said at last. 'They— I don't know—seem to find me too independent. I have thought I was in love a couple of times but it came to nought.' She shrugged.

'You—' He stopped as there was another crash, followed by a gunshot and a crescendo of angry voices.

Jo closed her eyes and turned her face into his shoulder as she trembled down the length of her.

He stroked her hair, but she could feel the tension, and the anger in him as well.

'Tell me about you,' she said shakily.

'Me? Well, I thought my life was perfect. I inherited Kin Can, I married the girl of my dreams, we made a baby and—it all fell apart because of an obscure medical condition no one realized my wife was suffering from that took her life just after Rosie was born.'

'I'm so sorry.' Jo clung to him as there was another shot and two crashes. It sounded as if they were wrecking the house. 'Go on.'

'There's not a lot more to tell. Rosie is the light of my life, I can't see myself ever marrying again—and do you think the bastards are killing each other?'

'I hope so, but why wouldn't you ever marry again?'

'I guess, once you've had perfection you just know it's an impossible act to follow. I guess I know myself well enough to know that I'd be holding every other woman up against that...happiness and finding her wanting. I suspect part of me will never forgive fate for what it did to me—and I'm a bad loser.'

'Do you have friends?'

He grimaced. 'I used to. All my friends are married now and they seem to specialize in trying to set me up with blind dates so I'm a bit wary of them. But, actually, my best friend married my sister, so I now have him as a brother-in-law.'

Jo opened her mouth, then shuddered against him as the fracas outside continued.

'What are your favourite things, Jo? Other than drawing? I—' he paused, then grinned '—for example, can't resist roast beef—never, ever eat lamb if I can avoid it. I'm particularly attached to my dogs, an ice-cold beer on a hot day and Nicole Kidman.'

Jo had to smile. 'Let's see, Hugh Grant and Colin Firth run a dead heat for me, chocolate and, above all, I love drawing kids.'

'Why? Don't they squirm and scratch?'

'Yes, but if you get them talking, they tell you wonderful things, their imaginations are marvellous. Although their parents would be horrified at some of the things you hear.'

'I can imagine. Have you had much to do with kids?'

'Uh-huh, especially foster-kids. I—have a very soft spot for them, of course, but all kids really. You often learn a lot from them.'

He hugged her hard, then sat up, drawing her nearer as the noise outside drew closer to their door. 'Time to remember I'm not a good loser,' he said grimly. 'I've just had a spark of inspiration. Why the *bloody* hell didn't I think of it earlier?'

'I don't know. What is it?'

He released and looked upwards. 'There's a man-hole in the ceiling.'

Jo followed his gaze. It was an old, iron-pressed ceiling with floral wreaths all over it, beautifully restored. 'Where? I can't see it.'

He pointed to a corner and gradually she made out a square cut into the iron, but her first instinct was that it would be impossible for them to get through it, manacled together as they were.

'We can do it, Jo,' he said when she voiced her concerns. 'All we have to do is push the dresser underneath and climb onto it. If you just follow my orders, we'll be fine.'

She gazed at him, then blew her fringe up with a smile in her eyes. 'Orders?'

'Well, instructions.'

'That's better. But,' she added as he grimaced, 'assuming we do, and don't get caught in the process, how will it help us? Surely they'll hear us moving about the roof? And what if they decide to accept your offer?'

Gavin Hastings rubbed his jaw. 'I could do it on my own,' he said reflectively. 'I've had a bit of practice at crawling around confined spaces soundlessly.'

'How so?'

'Spent some time in the SAS,' he said briefly. 'OK, we'll reserve it for desperation tactics at this stage.' He stopped as footsteps approached the door, and Jo clung to his hand.

'Listen—' he lowered his voice '—whatever happens now, do *exactly* as I say, Jo. Promise?'

She swallowed and nodded.

'The other thing is, there only seems to be one gun between them so whoever is toting it is the guy to be specially wary of, OK?'

She nodded again as the door was flung open.

There were only two of them—no sign of the tall man they'd attempted to bargain with, and that struck more terror into Jo's heart. Had they shot him when he'd tried to talk reason to them?

'Well, Gav,' the man who'd shot his way into the hut jeered, 'how much loose cash do you have stashed here?'

Jo breathed a tiny sigh of relief, although she felt a tremor of savage emotion course through the man she was manacled to.

But he said coolly enough, 'About three thousand dollars.'

The man jerked his head. 'Lead us to it, lover boy!'

Five minutes later, in what was obviously his study,

Gavin Hastings unlocked a cabinet and removed a cash box from it. He took a wad of hundred-dollar bills out of the box and laid the money on an impressive oak desk.

There was a short interlude while it was counted then shoved into the spokesman's pocket. The other man had said nothing and was clearly having trouble staying on his feet.

'Right. Hold up your hands,' the first man said, and when they did so he unlocked the handcuffs. 'There.' He stood back for a moment as they freed themselves but Jo knew that something was wrong. She could only see his eyes, but they had a glazed, un-with-it look that was terrifying and his whole stance was suggestive of a suppressed, horrible glee.

It only took a moment for her instinct to be proved right as their tormentor raised his gun and aimed it squarely at her.

And he said, not taking his eyes off her, 'See here, Gav, we decided there was no reason only you should be so lucky in...*lurve*, so we're taking this bit of hot stuff with us. Now don't you try and stop us, mate, otherwise she'll buy it.'

There was an instant of awful silence. Then Gavin erupted like a coiled spring. He knocked Jo backwards so she fell against the other man and knocked him off his feet. Then he launched himself at the first man—and the gun went off.

Jo shrieked in despair as she picked up a heavy marble antique inkwell and threw it at the man on the floor behind her. He'd been trying to get to his feet, but as the inkwell caught him on the temple he went out like a light.

Jo grabbed it up off the floor and turned to the melee struggling in front of her, which comprised Gavin Hastings and the man with the gun, and she bore down on them with the inkwell raised above her head and something like a banshee cry issuing from her lips.

But Gavin sat up abruptly and put out a hand. 'It's all right, Jo. I've knocked him out.'

She lowered the inkwell. 'Oh, thank heavens,' she breathed. 'So who got...?' Her voice rose as she noticed the blood dripping down his fingers. '*You* got shot! Oh, no!' She sank to her knees beside him. 'No, no, no!'

'I think it's only a flesh wound in my upper arm.' He grimaced and felt through his jumper cautiously.

'But you saved my life! You actually threw yourself in front of the gun. How can I ever repay you for that and what will I do if you die?' she gabbled, her face paper-pale and her grey eyes dark with disbelief and emotion.

'I'm not going to die, Josie.' He pulled his jumper over his head and Jo winced at the sight of the wound in his upper arm. But she immediately pulled off her tracksuit top and then the long-sleeved vest-top she wore beneath it, which she ripped into strips with her teeth and fingernails, then applied them as a pad and pressure bandages to his wound.

Gavin Hastings flinched but there was a suggestion of humour in his eyes as they rested on her, her upper body clad only in a bra as she worked on the dressings.

'What can you do to repay me, Jo? I think it would be a damn good idea if you married me.' He swayed suddenly, and blacked out.

CHAPTER FOUR

LATER that day, Gavin Hastings stirred in his hospital bed, where he'd been air-lifted by helicopter, and examined his disinclination to allow the sedative he'd been given to take effect.

He'd undergone a minor operation to have the bullet removed from his arm and received the good news that the bone hadn't been splintered. He'd been visited by his mother, who'd then flown on to Kin Can to take charge. She might have a memory like a sieve these days, but when she was in control mode she was highly effective.

Which was not to say she hadn't wept a couple of tears over him to think how close he'd come to dying, but she'd recovered swiftly, and had left him saying, 'All's well that *ends* well, darling!'

But had it ended?

He moved again, trying to get comfortable without disturbing the drip in his arm.

You can't ask someone to marry you, and *mean* it, only to black out before she's had a chance to answer, and say it's ended, he told himself.

When he'd come to, it had been to find himself in a chopper on the way to hospital with no sign of Jo, who'd been left behind at the station.

But why was he so sure he'd meant it? he pondered.

Why not say, for example—I think it would be a

damn good idea if you came to bed with me, Jo Lucas, because I've wanted you since you got rid of your anorak and your strides and revealed those lovely clean lines as well as an awful wrath at being importuned like that....

Not the time and place, of course, he reasoned, but perhaps more accurate than telling her he wanted to marry her?

No.

The negative stood out starkly in his mind. For whatever reason, and there were plenty—she was brave, proud, dignified, quietly humorous at times—it was marriage he wanted. But were any of those the right reasons?

They were certainly not the reasons he'd married Rosie's mother. Not the earth-shattering joy of knowing, for whatever reason, you were wildly, madly in love.

He rubbed his jaw. He'd been a lot younger then—when they'd first met at least, he and Sasha. Maybe maturity and the middle-thirties made you see things differently?

Maybe looking for love, as he'd done at times after Sasha's death, had produced a certain cynicism in him—of course it had!—with himself as much as anything.

So why—he gritted his teeth—did he have this firm conviction he needed to marry Jo Lucas? Especially after telling her he never intended to marry again as no other woman could ever match up to his dead wife.

Rosie, he thought suddenly, and his mother, Adele. Did the seeds of this lie with them?

It was true that, for the last couple of years, Rosie

had been unable to understand why she didn't have a mother like all her friends and her cousins. It was true Adele had been a godsend, but how fair was it to her to keep her tied to Kin Can for Rosie for ever?

Especially, now he came to think of it, after she'd established her own life in Brisbane several years after his father had died, and seemed to thrive on it.

It was that life, after all, that called her back to Brisbane so often, and it had been no problem to take Rosie with her. But Rosie started school next year, so hopping off with her grandmother frequently was not going to be possible, unless she moved to Brisbane with Adele for the school term and spent the holidays on Kin Can.

How did he feel about that?

And—why the hell hadn't he thought of this before?—did Adele feel she'd done her stint at Kin Can and deserved to retire gracefully? Was that why her time on the station was spent—he gritted his teeth again—redecorating until there was no corner of the house that hadn't been remodelled, repainted, re-upholstered or re-carpeted? Because otherwise the life bored her now? She wasn't a born country woman, he recalled.

'I see,' he said to himself. 'All this has been lurking at the back of your mind but you've been too damned arrogant to let it see the light of day or—too bloody *something* to admit you need a wife! You need a mother for Rosie, you need to allow your own mother her freedom, and who better than a girl who likes, admires and sounds as if she understands kids?

'At the same time, a girl you want as you haven't wanted anyone for a long time?'

CHAPTER FIVE

A FEW days later Jo stopped what she was doing—attempting to capture Adele Hastings in oil crayons—and sank her chin onto her hand as she recalled the wash-up of the abortive kidnap attempt.

Immediately after Gavin had asked her to marry him, he'd blacked out and a police helicopter had landed on the lawn.

What had transpired was that Gavin's mother had flown into Brisbane, only to suddenly remember Jo's imminent arrival on Kin Can. So she'd tried to ring the station in vain over a couple of days and finally got worried enough to ring the police.

They'd driven out from Cunnamulla and, on finding the Kin Can sign mysteriously removed, they'd called for back-up.

Gavin had been airlifted to hospital, and all three kidnappers—the tall one had also been shot but only wounded—had been taken into custody. A stash of drugs had been found in their van.

Case, the head stockman, had been liberated from a shed a few kilometres from the homestead.

The next day the silver-grey Range Rover driven by 'Joe' had been found to be stolen, which had made sense of the kidnappers' request for verification of what vehicle he'd be driving.

Even more sense to it all had come when the man who had wielded the gun had been discovered to be the brother of a Kin Can employee Gavin had sacked for incompetence and drug addiction. Revenge had been the motive for it all.

Jo had refused the police offer of hospitalization and counselling. Her worst problem, or so she'd thought, was only some spectacular bruising inflicted by Gavin himself when he'd tackled her to the floor in the boundary hut. She'd also been pressed into staying on by Gavin's mother, who'd flown into Kin Can later that day after visiting her son in hospital.

Rosie had been left in Brisbane with Gavin's sister in case the damage to the homestead, the police presence and the absence of her father might upset her.

It wasn't until the next day that Jo was able to ask Adele Hastings why she hadn't told her son about her portrait.

Adele struck an attitude of considerable hauteur— she was a petite, stylish redhead in her late fifties— and she informed Jo that the less Gavin was consulted about anything, the better.

Jo blinked and frowned. 'Why?'

'My dear, he has enough delusions of power as it is. So I usually go ahead and do my own thing, then when it's a *fait accompli*, he simply has to live with it.'

'But why would he object to you having your portrait done, Mrs Hastings?'

'He probably wouldn't have. It's the principle of the matter,' Gavin's mother confided. 'But you see, I also have a secret agenda, Joanne.'

They were having coffee poured from a Georgian silver pot into wafer-thin china cups despite sitting at the kitchen table. Adele, Jo was increasingly to discover, didn't believe in slumming it under any circumstances and the only reason they were in the kitchen was because there were police and workmen all over the rest of the house.

'A secret agenda?'

Adele Hastings eyed Jo over the rim of her cup out of blue eyes very much like her son's. 'Well, I planned to give *my* portrait to my daughter, Sharon, for her thirtieth birthday. She's a bit of a connoisseur and has expressed an interest in your work. She also has everything that opens and shuts so...' She waved an elegant hand. 'But it's Gavin I particularly want you to do. And maybe Rosie, if you have the time. But I especially want Gavin to hang up beside his father, grandfather and great-grandfather.'

Jo put her cup down with a slight clatter. 'Would he approve?'

'I doubt it. I mentioned it once and he said—forget it, he couldn't be bothered! You'd have to do it secretly, without sittings and so on. But I believe you're very clever like that, my dear,' Adele said warmly. 'My friend, Elspeth Morgan—she was the one who recommended you—was so impressed with all the portraits you did of her cats—from photos, apparently!'

Jo closed her eyes briefly. The Elspeth Morgan commission had been a nightmare, although a lucrative one. A formidable Brisbane society matron, she'd changed her mind six times about what clothes and jewels she should be captured for posterity wearing. Then she'd decided to get her four cats done individually as well, and been quite hurt when Jo had drawn the line at cat sittings and insisted on taking photos.

'Uh—I feel a sort of moral obligation not to draw people who expressly don't want to be done, Mrs Hastings.'

Blue eyes engaged with level grey ones. 'I see,' Adele said consideringly.

And, unbeknownst to Jo, Adele found herself recalling her son Gavin's strictures on the subject of Joanne Lucas.

Obviously in pain and looking feverish against a starched hospital pillowslip, he had nevertheless issued a series of instructions to her. No interviews to be given to the press; no press to be allowed on Kin Can at all, even only to photograph; Rosie to be kept in the dark and in Brisbane until he was up and about—and Jo Lucas to be kept on the station until he got back.

'How can I keep her if she doesn't want to stay?' she'd objected, looking mystified. 'It all sounds like a ghastly experience so it's understandable if she—'

'Beloved, use your considerable powers of persuasion,' he'd broken in with a half-smile, and added, as she'd looked more mystified, 'There are some things I need to—make up to her. I thought she was part of the gang at first. Just don't let her go.'

Adele Hastings withdrew her mind's eye from her wounded but still high-handed son and studied the young woman sitting across the table from her with a suddenly accelerated heartbeat. Was there something between them? Had Gavin fallen in love when she'd given up nearly all hope of it ever happening again? What sort of a girl was she?

Good bone structure, good figure if you liked tall girls, fine skin, lovely hair, but not, one would have thought, Gavin's type—why? Too…understated? Compared to the glorious vivacity, the dark flashing eyes, the bundle of fun and essential willowy chic Sasha, Rosie's mother, had been? Perhaps, but all the same…

Adele smiled suddenly with all the considerable charm she was capable of. 'Forget I even mentioned it, Joanne. But you will stay with us and at least do me and Rosie? One thing I do know, he would love a portrait of her. Not only that, I would just love you to be my guest!'

Jo stirred. 'Well—'

'There's also the fact,' Adele hastened on, 'that I feel so guilty about landing you in what happened, but lately I seem to have become quite scatter-brained!' She shook her head sorrowfully.

Jo found that she couldn't help warming to Gavin's mother. 'It's just as well you and Rosie weren't here at the time,' she said. 'Uh…'

'Please, Jo—may I call you that? And may I tell you a secret? My dear friend, Elspeth Morgan, is actually an old bat and for some reason your portrait of her and her damn cats has really turned her head. She's lording it over all of us like royalty and I can't bear to be outdone like that!'

Jo's lips twitched. 'Us?'

'We, a group of us, work on several charities together. She's always been something of a Hyacinth Bucket amongst us but now she's unbearable.'

Jo had to laugh. 'Thank heavens I didn't think of that at the time! I'd have made her look as if she'd stepped right out of *Keeping Up Appearances*.'

'So you'll stay?'

'Yes.'

'Lovely!' Adele sat back. 'Now just tell me what you need and I'll see you're as comfortable as possible.'

That had been three days ago, Jo recalled as she sat at the table in her bedroom late in the afternoon.

Unlike the bedroom she and Gavin had been locked into, this one was modern, spacious and minimalist. That was why she'd opted for it on being given a choice. There were no frills, although plenty of comfort and luxury beneath its cream and olive décor, and plenty of room for the large table that had been moved in for her to work at.

All the same, it had been three days of coming to understand that the kidnapping affair had taken more out of her than she'd anticipated. Three days of being cosseted by Gavin's mother, of giving statements to the police, and being shown round Kin Can.

Days of being unable to draw a thing.

And days in which to ponder the fact that her heart had actually tripped when Gavin Hastings had declared that it would be a damn good idea if she married him.

Not only had her heart tripped but no amount of telling herself it was only a joke, no amount of tossing and turning at night had been able to alter one simple little fact.

From hating Gavin Hastings, she'd gone, in the space of a heartbeat, to acknowledging she had finally fallen in love. Why it had happened, how it had happened—surely not simply because he'd thrown himself in front of a gun aimed at her? But she couldn't take issue with it either, not from her point of view. She could no longer think of him without the knowledge of love in her heart, and a quiver of desire throughout her body.

From his point of view, however, there was plenty with which to take issue. *Had* he only said it in a moment of light relief after appalling tension?

Jo, she told herself, not for the first time, of course he did. Only hours earlier, if that, he gave you, chapter and verse, every good reason why he wouldn't ever marry again. And it's no good telling yourself that if things could change rather like lightning tearing apart your soul for you, the same had happened for him.

'So why am I here?' she asked aloud. 'He's due home today and very shortly, and I should have shaken the dust of Kin Can off my shoes. Not only that, I can't draw a thing because all I want to draw—is him.'

She sat perfectly still for a few minutes. The house was quiet, she was alone in it apart from the housekeeper, Mrs Harper, who worked efficiently and discreetly, she'd discovered. Adele had flown to Brisbane to pick up Rosie and they were to collect Gavin from the Charleville base hospital on their way home.

She got up presently and wandered through the main rooms. Gavin Hastings had been right. His mother, if it was she and not his wife who'd decorated Kin Can homestead, had very superior ideas, not to mention long pockets.

The original farmhouse had obviously been renovated and considerably enlarged. Although there were some wonderful antiques around, modern touches had been introduced and some of them looked rather new. The formal lounge was spacious with deep white cut-velvet settees on a cinnamon carpet and a huge, glorious gold and dusky pink painting on a feature wall—just swirls of colour but riveting all the same.

Jo recognized the work of a Sydney artist and had a pretty accurate idea of the value of the painting—not small change by any means.

The dining room was starkly simple. Rattan chairs, a round glass table on a brass pedestal, a cream carpet, a gorgeous chandelier strung quite low and a huge pottery urn in one corner. But her favourite room was the one Adele called the garden room. It was a long converted veranda with sliding glass windows down its length and linen blinds.

There were basket chairs, indoor plants in terracotta tubs and low tables stacked with books and magazines. There were Mexican rugs on the polished wooden floor and a lovely view of the sparkling pool outside. It was surrounded by an emerald lawn fringed with flowerbeds and a variety of gums, white, red and yellow-barked.

You could be forgiven for forgetting you were in the midst of thousands of hectares of rather flat, arid-looking mulga country—the stunted acacia that nevertheless provided shade for sheep—when you gazed out onto this view, Jo mused. And she shook her head to think of how a virtual cloudburst only days ago had now been absorbed into the soil as if it had never happened.

But on the other side of the house there was ample evidence this was a working sheep station. A huge machinery shed dominated the landscape, plus—possibly the crux of it all—the shearing shed and attendant yards.

Jo had been given a tour of it all by Case. Despite their utilitarian purposes and the evidence that quad bikes had replaced, to some extent, horseback sheep-mustering, she'd felt an almost Banjo Paterson sense of romance. Especially when she'd been introduced to the working dogs, mostly border collies and kelpies.

To be the mistress of it all would be rather like being mistress of an empire.

The thought had crossed her mind while she'd patted a grinning border collie, taking her unawares and shaking her composure considerably. I must be mad, had been her next thought.

A couple of days later, as she stood under the archway leading to the garden room, she heard a light plane buzzing over the homestead, and her nerves tightened. The Hastings clan was due to land shortly. No more mad notions, Jo, she cautioned herself.

It hadn't been the ordeal Jo had somehow expected, meeting Gavin Hastings again. Of course his bubbly mother with her super social skills had helped. And his daughter, Rosie, had turned out to be a charming imp with her father's dark hair but someone else's dark eyes.

So, unless anyone had been particularly on the lookout, they wouldn't have noticed her slightly heightened colour or the evidence of what her heartbeat was doing, and she felt that, otherwise, she'd been relaxed and friendly about it all.

Then Adele had confided that she'd ordered a celebration dinner but they'd be having it early on account of Rosie, and they'd all gone to their rooms to change. Jo had passed through the dining room on her way to her room, to see the table set with silver, crystal and fine bone china, so she'd showered and changed into the best clothes she'd brought.

These were a fine silky-knit pewter top that crossed over her breasts and tied at the waist, a paler grey, three-quarter-length skirt and silver sandals. She put her hair up in a loose knot, changed her mind and took it down, then resolutely pinned it up again.

Relaxed and casual she might have been able to project on re-meeting Gavin Hastings, but inside her something seemed to be spinning...

'So—' Gavin handed Jo a nightcap, and a flicker of humour chased through his eyes, '—alone at last.'

She glanced up at him and accepted the drink. It wasn't that late but Rosie, complaining bitterly, had been taken to bed and Adele had retired to what she called her 'suite'.

'Are you fine now?' she queried as the silence began to stretch between them. They were in the garden room. Outside, the pool was lit and the trees around the perimeter of the lawn were casting some fascinating shadows.

'More or less. Some stitches to come out, that's all. What have you been up to?'

'Trying to draw, but not successfully. I really think I should have gone back to Brisbane—for a break at least—but your mother was very determined to have me stay.' She blew her fringe up.

Gavin Hastings paced up and down the polished floor then stopped to stare out at the pool as a wallaby hopped across the lawn. 'I told my mother to keep you here.'

Jo narrowed her eyes, then pleated her skirt. There was nothing to minimize his effect on her now.

In well-pressed khaki trousers, polished brown deck shoes and a red and white checked shirt there wasn't anything of a demented bushranger about him other than the remnants of his black eye. He also looked relaxed, although perhaps a little pale, but he had undergone an operation to remove the bullet from his arm.

As she mulled over what he'd said a faint smile replaced her frown as she studied her glass.

'What?' he queried.

She looked up to see him standing right in front of her with a question in his eyes.

She shrugged. 'I gather that being shot hasn't diminished your habit of being in command.'

'There was no reason for you not to stay on, was there?'

'How would you know?' she countered.

He pulled up a chair and sat down opposite her. 'Tell me about it. I thought you intended to stay on Kin Can for a couple of weeks at least.'

Jo gestured. 'Perhaps. But it was all rather traumatic. That—' she glanced at him quizzically '—didn't occur to you?'

'Jo—' he paused and their gazes locked '—I meant it. Will you marry me?'

She froze, then placed her glass carefully on a side table. 'Gavin, you couldn't possibly have meant it.

We barely know each other, we both have very good reasons for—'

'We know each other a hell of a lot better than most people,' he broke in. 'What we went through was extremely revealing, wouldn't you say?'

His eyes searched hers until she looked away.

'We also happen to want each other,' he added softly. 'Would you like me to tell you *how* I want you?'

'No,' she said swiftly and swallowed.

He grinned fleetingly. 'You couldn't stop me.'

'I…I could get up and go away,' she pointed out.

'Not very far. Assuming I allowed you to go anywhere.'

'Gavin—' some steel entered her grey gaze '—you used that tactic before, but may I point out you don't have a gun to reinforce it now?'

He grimaced. 'A gun with no bullets.'

'I wasn't to know that.'

'No, you weren't,' he agreed. 'Nor did it stop you from testing my intentions with the damn gun.'

'Well, then.' She folded her hands.

'I don't see why we can't have an adult conversation about it,' he said submissively.

Her gaze sharpened again, this time with acute suspicion, and his next words confirmed her suspicions—it was a highly unlikely state of mind to find him in…

'My mother didn't have a gun to hold to your head, bullet-less or otherwise.'

His words sank into a pool of silence but the inference was loud and clear—why *was* she still on Kin Can if she didn't want to be?

Jo bit her lip.

'See what I mean?' His blue eyes held a trace of ironic enquiry.

'Just as your mother feels you suffer from delusions of power, Gavin Hastings, she is also a powerful persuader.'

'So it had nothing to do with me?'

'Look—' she turned her head to stare out over the lawn for a long moment '—we both know exactly why marriage is not for us and none of those reasons has changed so—'

'Jo—' his voice hardened '—things do change and sometimes when you least expect them to. OK, yes, I fully expected the memory of Sasha to make it impossible for me to marry again, but this is different.'

'How could it be?' she asked with difficulty. 'How could you hold me up against her memory and *not* find me wanting? Tell me something.' It was a shot in the dark but something Adele had let drop forced her to make it. 'Who does Rosie remind you of vividly?'

'Her mother,' he said grimly. 'She always will. That doesn't mean you and I can't create our own world, our own magic. But let's talk about you for a moment.'

He paused, but gazed at her narrowly until she took refuge from his scrutiny by sipping her drink.

As he watched her it occurred to Gavin Hastings to find it incredible that he'd ever thought her unfeminine, even if so briefly.

All the same, seeing her dressed up for the first time was a sheer pleasure. Her sense of style might be understated but the pewter of her top highlighted her creamy skin and made her eyes greyer. As always the gold of her hair was gorgeous, although he objected to it being tied up, he discovered.

Then there were those legs. Her thigh was sculpted by her skirt as she sat, turned a little away from him, and her ankles were slim and elegant in high-heeled sandals.

'Know what I thought while I was in hospital?' he said at last.

She shook her head.

'I thought if, when I get home, Jo Lucas has gone, that'll be her way of telling me it's no go. But if she's still there, it'll be because she's…at least curious…to see if I meant it.'

Jo stared at him with her lips parted.

'Mmm… Not only curious to see if I meant it,' he went on, 'but unable to shake off the physical and mental closeness we shared over those awful hours, the trust we shared while we were manacled together. Believe me, there could hardly be anything more claustrophobic than being handcuffed to a guy you hate and mistrust.'

'You…' She licked her lips. 'You were on the good side.'

'Maybe.' His eyes bored into her own.

'And, of course,' she added in case that sounded ungrateful, 'you did save my life at the possible expense of your own.'

He smiled faintly and shook his head.

'You didn't?' Her eyes widened.

'It was a calculated risk that went slightly wrong. I had no intention of either of us getting shot. My reflexes must have been a bit out of training. Mind you, the science of calculated risks is always—a risky business.'

Jo released a slow breath. 'Whether it was a calculated risk or not, it was still extremely brave and I'm still extremely grateful.'

'Good.' His lips twisted. 'Why don't you apply that thinking to what I could do for you if you married me?'

She stood up abruptly and tossed him a rather tart little look.

'Don't trade too much on that, Gav Hastings,' he murmured, 'in other words?'

This time the look she shot him shouted, You better believe it!

He laughed softly. 'That's my Josie! Anyway—' he stood up '—think about it.'

Surprise caused her to blink before she said cautiously, 'Does that mean I'm off the hook for the moment?'

He shoved his hands in his pockets. 'Of course. Never let it be said I pressured you into anything. Incidentally, if you're worried about your career as an artist, I think it's very appropriate for a wife.'

Jo opened and closed her mouth several times like a fish out of water.

'And talking of thinking about things, there is always this.' His eyes glinted as he moved to stand beside her. 'Definitely worth thinking about, I would have thought.'

She knew in the split second before he did it what was coming, but *her* reflexes let her down. Indeed, she found she couldn't move a muscle as he took her in his arms.

'I wonder if you have any idea,' he said, barely audibly, 'how your mouth tempts me, Miss Lucas?'

'Why?' She frowned in genuine puzzlement.

'Why? It's just luscious and asking to be kissed, that's why. Hasn't anyone told you that?'

She shook her head. 'I…don't much enjoy being kissed.'

'Could be you haven't met the right man yet.' His eyes glinted. 'Have you ever experienced an orgasm?'

Jo opened her mouth to tell him it was none of his business, but changed it to, 'Why?' again.

He frowned faintly. 'I get mixed signals. There's this cool, calm Jo Lucas quite capable of holding her own against any man, one feels, then there's the cuddly girl who slept in my arms and really didn't want to leave them—'

'So that's what you were so smug about!'

'Bastard that I am,' he agreed without the least trace of repentance. 'But there's also—I don't know—something that makes me wonder.' He frowned again.

'If I'm some kind of freak?' she suggested dryly. 'I'm surprised you want to marry me, in that case.'

'Not at all. The prospect of being man enough to do it is highly appealing,' he said seriously.

Jo caught her breath, because this was absolute arrogance if nothing else and therefore intolerable, but just as she was about to tell him so he started to laugh.

'You thought I was serious, Josie!'

Colour flooded her cheeks and he took advantage of her confusion to lower his mouth to hers.

'Won't hurt in the slightest,' he promised against her lips. 'Just leave it to me.'

Far from hurting or being the invasion she'd always found distasteful, it was increasingly fascinating. Then again, Gavin Hastings took his time about really kissing her. He nuzzled the corner of her mouth, her cheek, the side of her throat at the same time as he swept his hands slowly but, oh, so thoroughly down her body.

At the same time, he drew her against him and she had to fight against a deliciously sensuous tide that flooded her at the contact with his warm, hard body.

Then he curved one hand round the back of her neck and began to explore her breasts with the other.

She breathed raggedly.

'Nice?' His lips returned to the corner of her mouth.

She didn't answer, she couldn't find the words to tell him it might be nice but it was also dangerous. But she did find herself hanging onto his arm unexpectedly, until he lifted his head suddenly and grimaced in pain.

'Oh!' Her hand flew to her mouth. 'Your wound—I'm so sorry!'

'It's OK. Here—' he repositioned them so a wall was behind her '—lean back.'

'Why?'

'Just so I can get my breath again.'

'But I feel terrible,' she protested.

'Jo—' he brought both hands up to imprison her between them against the wall '—I'm fine. And all the more fine to be doing this. Just relax.' This time, he lowered his mouth to tease her lips apart.

She did relax, mainly because she was still concerned about hurting him and not wanting to do it again. Or, she wondered, was it an urge to heal the hurt she'd caused that made her really let her guard down?

Whatever, she went from being wary about the way he was arousing her to accepting it. The next step, allowing her senses to participate, came swiftly. Her skin shivered when he moved one hand from the wall to slide it down her arm. Then his fingers moved to her throat and slipped down to the V opening of her top.

She caught her bottom lip between her teeth, and moved forward against him. His other hand came down and he wrapped his arm around her, and she breathed deeply. As she did so the last of her wariness dissolved completely beneath an assault of pure pleasure and pure man.

'Did you know,' he said at one stage, 'that you looked very attractive tonight but stern? I much prefer you like this.'

'Like what?' she breathed.

'Disordered and wanton.'

'I'm no such thing!'

His hands moved deftly and he released her hair from its knot and untied her top. 'No?'

'That's your doing, not mine,' she protested, but with little heat.

He smiled lazily. 'I've been thinking of doing it for days. You do realize that even while I was harbouring the deepest suspicions about you, Jo, I was—unable to keep my mind off your body and all its delights?'

'I did realize—' she moved beneath his exploring fingers '—that you were being rather bloody-minded about women and their intentions, mine in particular.'

He laughed softly and pushed her top back to kiss her shoulder. 'I hope this is a suitable form of revenge.'

She raised her arms and ran her fingers through his hair, then drew her hands down his back. 'Revenge?'

'Mmm...' He slipped her bra strap aside. 'You have me at your mercy at the moment, Miss Lucas.'

She opened her mouth to say that it could be the other way around, but he forestalled her.

'Or, maybe it's mutual.' And this time, as he cupped her breast he started to kiss her in earnest.

She kissed him back. For the first time in her life she really gave herself up to being kissed and was almost unbearably pleasured by the unexpected intimacy of it.

Her senses spun and she couldn't stay still. She couldn't get enough of the fire and heat of his body on hers and his touch on her breasts and hips seemed to brand her and claim her for his own, almost as if she were his creation.

And she was, she realized. This tall man who'd started out by insulting her in just about every conceivable way, then saved her life whether he liked to think it or not, had somehow unlocked the essence of her femininity. So that she longed to beg for more intimacy, the closest no-holds-barred kind of all.

They drew apart at last and Jo had to lean back against the wall for support. He put his hands up to imprison her against it again and stared down at her.

Her gorgeous mouth was bruised and ripe. Her golden hair lay in a swathe across one shoulder with her fringe in her eyes. Her breasts heaved—there was a dew of sweat trickling down the smooth, pale valley between them until she, belatedly, pulled her bra up, and she blew up at her fringe.

For some reason they both smiled at this little reflex gesture of hers, and he decided to complete her restoration himself.

He combed her fringe aside with his fingers and retied her top, smoothing it into place, then he looked into her eyes again.

Her smile had gone and they were dark now, as if with shock, as if the magnitude of the experience was hitting her—or the unexpectedness of her response? he wondered.

And he realized in the same breath that it was going to take a lot of will power to defuse things between them. An almost inhuman effort, in fact, not to take her by the hand and lead her to his bed and keep her there until she shuddered in his arms and came beneath him...

Then she blinked several times as her gaze focused on the sleeve of his shirt, and he looked down to see a patch of blood.

At the same time Jo Lucas came out of her daze into a sudden fever of a different kind—concern.

'Oh, no! Look what I've done! Why didn't you say? I must be mad!'

'Believe me, I didn't feel a thing and you weren't mad at all.'

'Of *course* I was. So were you!' she retorted. 'How could you even think of going around kissing people like that with a gunshot wound in your arm?'

'I wasn't kissing people plural, only one. You,' he pointed out.

'Don't split hairs,' she warned. 'Let me have a look.'

She started to unbutton his shirt with a militant expression.

'I take it this is not a good time to argue with you, Jo?' he drawled.

'It isn't.' She eased his shirt off.

'Would you mind if I swore comprehensively?'

'Be my guest. I've no doubt heard it all before.'

'Ma'am, in that case I'll give it a miss.' He looked down at the dressing on his arm. 'It probably only needs replacing.'

'We'll see. Come with me.' She handed him his shirt and turned away.

He followed her to her en-suite bathroom where she retrieved her first-aid kit from a drawer. She then proceeded, with competence, to remove the dressing, swab the wound where it had opened slightly between stitches, and redress it.

'There.' She patted him lightly on the elbow. 'I don't think you did too much damage, but you should see a doctor if it keeps on bleeding.'

He put his shirt on with a frown in his eyes. 'Are you also a nurse?'

'No, but I did a first-aid course at school.'

'And did it very thoroughly, by the look of it.' His hands paused in the act of buttoning his shirt. 'Why do I get the feeling you do everything thoroughly, Jo Lucas?'

She raised her eyebrows. 'I have no idea.' She suddenly noticed that he'd buttoned his shirt crookedly and with a click of her teeth started to re-button it.

He put his hands on her wrists and stilled her busy fingers. 'See what I mean?' he murmured.

She lowered her lashes in some confusion.

He added, 'All the more reason to marry you.'

The bathroom had cream tiles and olive-green fittings. There was a wide mirror above the twin basins and Jo turned away from Gavin Hastings, to find herself looking into it, and getting a shock.

Her hair was a mess, her face was pale and her eyes looked different, although she couldn't say why. Then it hit her. They were completely bemused.

'That offer is still open, incidentally,' he said. 'Much as you've made a point of changing the subject.'

She stared at him in the mirror and thought of objecting that she'd had good cause. But perhaps there was a more pertinent objection to make?

'All this has happened so…so *fast*.'

'That's because of the way we met. High drama had an accelerating effect. We were sharing a toothbrush only hours after we'd been introduced. We were virtually sleeping together *before* that.'

She shook her head. 'We weren't!'

'No, you're right,' he agreed, 'now I come to think of it. You must have moved into my arms at least—two hours after I introduced myself?'

Jo looked away from the pure devilry in his eyes. 'You're never going to let me live that down, are you?'

'Nope. And, of course, there's the fact that I saw you stripped to your underwear only about five minutes after we met, Lady Longlegs,' he added softly.

Jo made an abrupt movement, then turned resolutely to face him. 'You can't just ask me to marry you like this without some…explanation. Not after what you said.'

'Jo—' he sobered abruptly '—I'm rushing my fences, aren't I? Sorry. The thing is, it suddenly came to me that I needed a wife because Rosie needs a mother and my mother needs a break. But *before* I worked that out, I had this—I don't know—conviction, that it needed to be *you*.'

'Why?' she whispered.

He shrugged. 'The link the whole kidnapping debacle forged between us? You may think I saved your life, but what you may have forgotten is the lengths you were about to go to with a solid marble inkwell to save mine. Perhaps it's that between us. We care about each other, Jo.'

'As opposed to being deeply, wildly, madly in love?'

She thought he flinched as she said the words, but might have imagined it.

'Sometimes the less flamboyant emotions are the ones with the better foundations.'

Her gaze dropped after what seemed like an eternity and she said very quietly, 'I'll think about it.'

He studied her and seemed about to say something, but changed his mind in the end, and dropped the lightest kiss on her hair before he turned away.

CHAPTER SIX

JO ELECTED not to go to bed immediately.

She pulled on a cardigan and let herself out onto the veranda from her bedroom, then down a short flight of wooden steps onto the lawn. This was not the pool side of the house but the garden was well tended and there were some lovely shrubs against the veranda wall.

There was also a bench and she sat down and hugged herself. Although it was starting to warm up as spring came to Kin Can, the night air was crisp and cold, there was no cloud cover to trap the warmer air of the day or hide the stars, and there were millions of them.

Due to the lack of artificial light, this area of Queensland was renowned for its view of the night sky.

She gazed upwards for a while, admiring the heavens on one level of her mind, but mostly preoccupied with the miracle that had happened to her tonight, the release from an experience that had coloured her whole life.

It was true she'd always found being kissed distasteful for one very good reason. Between twelve and eighteen, she'd lived with three foster families. Two of them had been warm, supportive and gone out of their way to make her feel part of the family. One of them had proved to be a nightmare.

She'd been fifteen when the husband had started to pay attention to her in a secretive, nauseating way. It had started out with compliments on her figure, then he'd started to touch her, accidentally, she'd thought at first, but one day he'd cornered her and kissed her, then issued a warning to her that if she told anyone, no one would believe her, against him, anyway.

She'd packed her bags and run away to the local police station from where she'd been passed on to the Department of Family and Community Services.

At first, no one *had* believed her, there had even been suggestions she might have 'led him on', but she'd stuck to the absolute truth, her record as a 'sensible' girl had come to her rescue and an investigation had been mounted. Two more girls had been found, who'd lived with the same family and had had similar experiences, although they'd been too scared to come forward at the time.

She'd refused point-blank to go on to any family with a man in the house, she'd received counselling and she'd ended up with a middle-aged widow with a social services background herself, and a daughter Jo's age who had become her best friend.

She'd overheard her counsellors agreeing once that she would most likely be able to put the whole experience behind her because she was so—thank heavens!—sensible, gutsy and independent.

They'd been wrong. They'd overlooked that she was also sensitive. It had lingered at the back of her mind ever since. Her memories had come between her and a couple of men she'd thought she might have fallen in love with.

Perhaps, even, the experience of not being believed

at first had been as damaging as anything else in that her independence had become crucial to her. Never again would she rely on anyone believing her or not.

Gavin Hastings had changed all that. Somehow he'd swept it away effortlessly. Because they'd become so close and shared such heart-stopping danger? Because he had thrown himself in front of a gun aimed at her whether he liked to think of it as a calculated risk or not? Because they'd confided in each other the way they had?

Whatever, even although her heartbeat had tripped when he'd suggested she marry him, nothing had prepared her for the flood of sensuality he'd released in her tonight.

She closed her eyes. She was purged at last. She'd fallen in love and she was loving it—only thing, how was she going to cope with the fact that deeply, wildly, madly might never happen again for him when she suspected it had already happened for her? How was her sensible, gutsy, stubborn independence, but also that innate sensitivity, going to cope with that?

CHAPTER SEVEN

THE next morning, Jo awoke to find Rosie sitting on the end of her bed.

'Good day.' She struggled up and peered at her bedside clock. It was six-thirty and daylight was just starting to filter through her windows.

'Hello!' Rosie said brightly. 'We always get up at the crack of dawn, I thought I'd let you know.'

'So I see.' Jo combed her hair with her fingers.

'Nanna says you're going to draw my portrait as well as hers. I'm so excited because I love to draw myself! Would you like to start now?'

'Now? Uh…' Jo trailed off.

'How about I get you a cup of tea? Nanna swears by her first cuppa.'

'Thank you, that would be lovely.'

Rosie went away and Jo showered swiftly. She was dressed by the time Rosie returned with a tray bearing, not only a cuppa but a glass of milk and two slices of toast.

'One for you, one for me,' she said of the toast, 'and the milk's for me. Mrs Harper did it for me, grumbling all the while that I had no right to wake you up so early, but since I had, she might as well make you some tea. I told her that inspiration waits for no man, but we might need something to keep the wolf from the door.'

Jo regarded Gavin Hastings's daughter—and felt

her fingers tingle in response to messages her brain was receiving. Rosie Hastings was a character.

Obviously used to a lot of adult company, she was very articulate but often sounded quaintly old-fashioned. She had also put on what looked like her best outfit, a pink, fine-corduroy, long-sleeved dress with a ribbon sash, white tights and she'd tied her long dark hair back in pigtails.

The presentation was slightly flawed—some of her buttons were undone, her sash was twisted and her hair a bit knotted—but she still looked like a little girl from a bygone era.

'Thank you,' Jo said gravely. 'I haven't had toast soldiers for a while.'

Rosie grinned. 'How would you like me to pose?'

Jo thought for a bit as she sipped her tea. 'Tell you what, since you love it, why don't you do some drawing? I'll give you some of my paper and you can use this second set of pencils I always carry.' She pointed to a smaller box on the table.

'What a great idea,' Rosie enthused. 'Now what shall I draw? I know! Dad's favourite dog had puppies the other day. Let's see if I can remember them.' She screwed up her face.

They drew for about half an hour and Rosie chatted all the time.

If she was the light of her father's life, Gavin was the adored hero of his daughter. Nanna featured as well and obviously was much-loved, but it was Gavin she talked about most. Rosie also indicated that she loved the station life and was very much looking forward to starting school, although she then sighed suddenly and propped her chin on her hands.

'What is it?' Jo asked.

'Well. There's complications.' And Rosie embarked on a multi-stranded explanation.

Apparently, her dearest wish was to join the School of Distance Education. Formerly known as the School of the Air, the local headquarters were in Charleville and she was already enrolled in their preschool.

Jo knew something about the School of Distance Education from her flatmate Leanne, who had worked on the project. She knew, for example, that the Home Tutor played a pivotal role. In the case of Kin Can, which had four school-age children not counting Rosie, Case's wife, Janine, an ex-schoolteacher, filled that role perfectly as well as being a very nice person. Three of the children were hers.

Jo also knew from Leanne what a vital role the school played, not only in educating outback children, but reaching into their isolated lives and bringing them together.

Rosie enlarged on this aspect. Just about every kid in the district she knew was or would be joining the school.

'I mean,' she said, 'I know that *one* day I'll have to go away to boarding school, but until then I want to be a part of the school. This is my home,' she added quaintly.

'Why not, then?'

'Nanna likes to spend a lot of time in Brisbane and I nearly always go with her, but I couldn't do that once I've started school, so she suggested I go to a school in Brisbane and we come back to Kin Can for holidays.'

'That doesn't appeal to you?'

'No. Of course, much as I love Nanna, if I had my *own mother* like every other kid I know, there wouldn't be a problem! It really is quite a blight on my life, Jo,' she confided gloomily.

Jo's pencil paused and remained poised above the paper. 'You seem to get along rather well with Mrs Harper. Couldn't she look after you while your nanna's in Brisbane?'

Gloom was replaced with flashing scorn. 'They won't even hear of it! Anyone would think I was a baby.'

'I see. What does your father say?'

Rosie deepened her voice. '"We've got months to think about it, catfish, and as Gavin Hastings the Fourth, I can be relied on to make the right decision."'

Jo had to laugh. 'Catfish?'

'It's a joke between us.' Rosie paused as there was a light knock on the door and it clicked open.

'Daddy!' Rosie jumped up and ran over to her father with her drawing. 'Look at this!'

'Rosie, what are you doing here at this hour of the morning? That's nice, but—' Gavin glanced at the drawing '—never again, it's too early. Morning, Jo! I'm sorry about this. For some reason I slept in myself.'

'It's OK,' Jo said. 'We have got to know each other a bit.'

Gavin narrowed his gaze on her rather unseeingly, as if searching back through his memory. 'What,' he said at last, 'has she been telling you?'

Jo smiled wryly. 'That's just between the two of us.'

Rosie looked approving. 'I like someone who can keep a secret. Is breakfast ready? I'm starving!'

The morning passed swiftly.

To Jo's relief, the flying doctor called in, on a clinic run, to check Gavin out.

'Listen, mate,' he admonished Gavin as he replaced Jo's dressing and was told the wound had bled a little, 'you've got to give it time to knit. What on earth were you doing?'

Jo held her breath.

'I was—rushing my fences,' Gavin replied, and shot her a wicked look. 'Speaking figuratively, of course.'

'Well, stop rushing damn fences, whatever that means. You're not in the SAS any more.' The doctor repacked his bag, then looked over at Jo, as if somehow he'd caught the vibes of the moment, and he raised his eyebrows.

'Uh—this is Joanne Lucas, Tom,' Gavin introduced. 'She's here to do Adele's portrait. Jo, meet Tom Watson.'

'Ah! The lady we've been hearing about. Good to meet you! I believe you were exceptionally brave in ghastly circumstances.'

'She was,' Gavin said before Jo could answer for herself. 'Therefore, I'm trying to persuade her to marry me.'

Tom laughed. 'I'd think twice about that if I were you, ma'am. Gavin, here, is renowned for getting his own way. OK, got to fly!' But he paused suddenly with a swift frown, then shook his head and climbed aboard his plane.

'How could you do that?' Jo enquired as they watched the trim RFDS plane taxi down the grassy airstrip.

'Do what?'

'*Tell* him you were thinking of marrying me—as if you didn't know.'

'He took it as a joke.'

Jo glinted him a dark little look. 'Then he stopped to think about it, just as he stopped to think about "rushing fences".'

Gavin grinned and took her hand. 'He's no fool, Tom. And it's no joke either.'

'Gavin—'

'Jo, can I make a suggestion?'

She looked at him warily.

'How would it be if we took a week or two to think this through? You could size up country life, size up my family—not to mention me—and you could do my mother's portrait.'

'I...'

'Is that so much to ask?'

'Do you mean—in return for saving my life?'

He gestured. 'No, of course not. Forget I ever said that. Incidentally, what did Rosie say to you this morning?'

Jo was debating whether to tell him when Rosie and Adele hove into view.

'All right,' he said, 'we'll leave that for a moment. Will you stay and case the joint?'

She smiled slightly. 'Gangster talk, Gavin?'

'It is how we met.'

She gazed at the dusty horizon. 'If you promise me one thing.'

'What's that?'

She looked into his eyes. 'If the answer is no, you'll take it.'

'Done,' he replied promptly. So promptly Jo was immediately suspicious.

'Do you mean that?'

'I am a man of my word.'

She frowned. 'Can I add a rider?'

'Let me guess,' he said gravely. 'Something to do with no—undue pressure?'

'Yes,' she agreed dryly.

'Jo, if you're embarrassed about the way you kissed me last night, don't be. It was enchanting,' he said simply.

She coloured.

'It was also as sexy as hell,' he added, 'and—'

'It's not that I'm embarrassed,' she broke in a little hastily. 'It's obviously a factor to take into account, but—'

'A major factor,' he put in, and lifted his hand to trace the outline of her mouth gently.

Jo trembled as she recalled, with breathtaking clarity, the feel of his hands on her breasts and hips. 'Your mother and daughter are nearly upon us,' she said with an effort.

He dropped his hand and glanced over his shoulder. 'OK. You tell me when you feel I'm exerting undue pressure. Is it a deal?'

It occurred to her she should have added all sorts of riders: no further mention of his proposal to others, no public displays of the attraction that existed between them were two that flashed though her mind. But all she had time to say was, 'Uh…yes.'

'Good.' He turned to greet Rosie and Adele.

Two weeks later the time had literally flown as she'd experienced a thorough but very enjoyable induction to the Hastings version of country life. Although, two things had worked in her favour regarding 'undue pressure' at least.

Gavin couldn't be involved in the more active things she did while his arm healed, and she was able to close herself into her room frequently on the pretext of working on his mother's and his daughter's portraits.

But he did spend time talking sheep to her. He told her how Kin Can was experimenting with a new concept—electronic tagging of individual sheep.

'How on earth could that work?' she asked.

He shrugged. 'Electronic tag readers collate information like weight, need for parasite control, et cetera, so you get a much more accurate picture of the sheep's condition.'

'Science is amazing, isn't it?' She shook her head in wonder. They were leaning against a fence watching a 'yarding'—sheep being sorted into different pens. The air was dusty and alive with whistles as the dogs worked their magic, and sheep proved their propensity for jumping over imaginary hurdles.

He eyed her. She wore jeans and a blue shirt and the breeze was lifting her hair.

'You're—' He stopped a little ruefully.

She looked a question at him.

'Er—I was going to make a remark of a personal nature but I could stick to sheep, it's up to you.'

She smiled fleetingly. 'Stick to sheep.'

'I don't know why I asked since I knew damn well that's what you would say,' he grumbled, but good-naturedly, and thought for a moment.

'All right, you asked for it. Fibre diameter is the key to lightweight comfortable woollen products—'

'You mean each hair?'

'I do. The lower the better, and that, amongst other reasons, is why we farm mostly Merino sheep for wool. Staple strength is another factor, so is rainfall, country and so on. The further south you get in the Queensland sheep belt, the lower the fibre diameter in general. Overall there are nine to ten million sheep in Queensland.'

He paused briefly. 'China is our biggest market for Queensland wool and Australia is the biggest producer in the world of "apparel" wool. An experienced shearer can shear one hundred and twenty to one hundred and forty sheep a day—'

'*What?*'

'It's true, but you've made me lose my train—uh—'

'Thank you,' she said gravely. 'I think that may be enough information to digest for the moment.'

'Are you sure? There's a lot more—'

'Gavin, I'm sure.'

'Then may I say you're amazingly attractive, Miss Lucas? That's all I was going to say in the first place,' he hastened to assure her.

Jo had to dissolve into laughter.

At other times, she learnt to drive a quad bike. She had some wonderful fun mustering sheep with Case, and getting used to all the whistles, calls and gestures needed to control the dogs.

She glowed when Case told 'the boss' she was a natural.

Rosie gave her a guided tour of the shearing shed, displaying remarkable knowledge as well as her love of station life. Rosie rode her own pony and was to be given one of the pups of the new litter as her own dog. The agony of which to choose was causing her a lot of concern.

Jo and Rosie used the pool most days, days that were warming up more and more, and anyway the pool was heated. Rosie was a dog-paddler and quite safe in the pool, but Jo was an accomplished swimmer and, in a couple of days, she had the little girl doing a passable breaststroke much to Rosie's delight—and her father's approval.

Her father's approval didn't only extend to Rosie's swimming, it extended to her coach. He had a way of examining Jo's figure in a halter-neck candy-striped swimming costume that spoke volumes. Especially when she was dripping wet and her nipples were clearly visible beneath the Lycra.

But all he actually said, and only on one occasion, when his daughter was out of earshot, was that legs that went on for ever were now high on his agenda of feminine perfection.

Jo had glinted him an enigmatic little look, and wrapped a towel around her waist so it covered her legs to her knees.

Not, she had to admit to herself, that she was immune from being tantalized by him. Talking of legs, he had a long-legged stride that was so essentially masculine, it fascinated her.

He also had a way of shoving his hand through his hair that indicated he was about to be exasperated and difficult, then a completely wicked little smile that told you he knew it but couldn't help himself. Everyone, she realized, from his foreman, his housekeeper, his mother, his daughter and herself included, tended to have the wind taken right out of their sails beneath that smile.

He was also incurably, she knew, used to getting his own way, but in one minor tussle she'd had with him, when she'd simply and calmly agreed to disagree with him, he'd looked so surprised for a moment, she'd had to resist a powerful urge to kiss him and tell him to be a good boy.

She'd learnt swiftly that that would not have been a good idea because he'd obviously read her thoughts.

He'd eyed her then, from head to toe, and murmured, 'Feeling maternal, Jo?'

'Well—'

'Believe me, that's not how I think of you. In fact I often wonder how you like to make love—soberly? Joyfully? Are you practical even in bed? Or generous? Does that lovely body—' his blue gaze stripped her naked '—arch and writhe and—ah!' He paused and studied the colour flooding her cheeks. 'Not motherly, then.'

She swung on her heel and marched away from him.

That night, as was happening to her more and more frequently, she couldn't help fantasizing about making love to Gavin. And it came to her that if just watching the way he walked and being seriously affected by it was any guide, 'sober' would probably not be how she would feel in his bed.

She learnt too, also from Gavin, more about the Hastings 'empire'. Not only did Kin Can produce wool, they bred rams that were sold all over the world, sometimes fetching staggering amounts of money. Then there were two adjacent cattle properties, a horse stud, Gavin's creation, a cane farm in North Queensland and a long list of commercial enterprises.

'You obviously don't believe in having all your eggs in one basket,' she commented as she studied a blown-up map of Queensland with the Hastings properties etched in a rich, royal blue.

They were in his study, a room she still associated with violence and mayhem, although it had been over three weeks ago.

He shrugged. 'You can't really afford to. Drought and flood, but particularly drought, plague this part of the world.'

She frowned. 'It does flood out here, though.'

'Oh, yes. In fact I have a feeling in my bones this season could be building up to it, but in general drought is much more common.'

'Go on,' she invited.

'Well, wool also has its ups and downs. Beef prices can be notoriously fickle, although we're cashing in nowadays. On the other hand, sugar, at the moment, is hard to give away. Which is why I'm toying with the idea of setting up some fish farms on the cane farm.'

'What about horses?'

'Yearling prices, well-bred yearlings at least, have sky-rocketed recently and I happen to have a couple of ''in vogue'' stallions.'

Jo studied him. He was lying back in a black leather swivel chair behind the oak desk looking big but relaxed, and as if all the power vested in him, as represented by the empire on the map in front of him, sat easily with him.

She frowned as she was struck by a sudden thought. 'Did you have any training to take on all this?' She gestured towards the map.

He crossed his hands behind his head. 'I was brought up to it. My father always believed in a very ''hands on'' approach, and he passed that on to me while I was growing up.'

'So you never wanted to do anything else?'

He grimaced. 'Not really.'

'What about the SAS?'

He lowered his hands and shrugged. 'It's a family tradition for sons to do a stint in the Services and I seemed to have the right qualities to get into the SAS, but I never intended to make the army a career. Then my father died—far too young, sadly—and I came back to take over. Been doing it ever since.' He regarded her thoughtfully. 'Do you have a problem with any of that?'

'No,' Jo said hastily.

He smiled. 'You're looking at me as if you suspect me of all sorts of vices.'

She shook her head and turned away. 'Excuse me, Adele has promised me a sitting.'

'How's it going?'

'Fine,' she said brightly.

'What did you do with my portrait?'

'I...I still have it. Why?'

'Just wondered. OK.' He glanced at his watch. 'See you at dinner. I believe we have company.'

Jo groaned. 'You do an awful lot of entertaining!'

'I don't, my mother does.'

'If I'd known I'd have brought more clothes.'

'You always look fine to me.' His gaze drifted down her figure, then moved up to capture her eyes.

'Thanks,' she said, and stirred uneasily.

'Does that come under the heading of "undue pressure"?' he queried wryly.

'No. No, you've been—apart from a couple of times you've been pretty good about that.' She flinched visibly as she said the words and flinched again as he laughed softly, his eyes alight with devilry, and he got up to come round the desk towards her.

'"Goodness" had nothing to do with it, not the way you occupy my thoughts, anyway. Great restraint plus the thought of having to explain to Tom why I'd opened up my stitches again is more accurate, Jo.'

'Oh.'

'How about you?'

She coloured.

'No restraint required?' His blue eyes were perfectly wicked.

'Some,' she conceded.

He lifted a hand as if to touch her, then hesitated and dropped it, and her body screamed in frustration, shocking her with the intensity of the arousal just the thought of his hands on her could evoke.

'Jo?'

She took a step backwards but he followed her, and she wondered dazedly what he would think if he knew that the only portrait going well for her was the one she worked on after everyone had gone to bed. Not Adele, not Rosie, but himself, stripped to the waist and sitting at an old wooden table in a shadowy hut.

The one she worked on from memory as she tried to add up what mattered most to her about Gavin Hastings.

Was that practising restraint? she wondered. Or was that indulging herself in a way she shouldn't if she decided not to marry him?

'What is it, Jo? Surely we can talk at the same time as you come to grips with the lifestyle?'

She bit her lip. 'Of course! Only not right now. Your mother—'

'Blow my mother.'

'Gavin, she is waiting for me.'

'Tonight, then.' He swore. 'After this blasted dinner party. Because I get the feeling you're tying yourself up in unnecessary knots, Jo Lucas. And what is not helping,' he added grimly, 'is this ridiculous rider about no undue pressure. What the hell do you think I'm liable to do to you? Seduce you out of your mind?'

A tinge of annoyance seeped into her veins. 'You wouldn't succeed. And I should warn you not to get too high-handed with me. I may have—' She broke off, then continued, 'I might like some things about you but I will never like that!'

'Or—you may have fallen in love with me, Josie?' he said softly. 'Is that what you were going to say?'

'Jo—oh, there you are!' Adele swept into the room. 'Did I get the time wrong? I was waiting in my sitting room.'

'I'm just on my way,' Jo said thankfully.

'Yes, why don't you toddle off?' Gavin Hastings invited dangerously.

'What's biting him?' Adele enquired as she settled herself in a lovely old oak abbot's chair.

'I have no idea,' Jo replied briefly, still simmering with annoyance as she organized herself.

Adele had given much thought to how she should be depicted in her portrait. And she'd come up with almost the exact opposite in the details to her friend Elspeth Morgan.

No jewels other than a black pearl ring, although it was the size of a pigeon egg, on her right hand. No off-the-shoulder colourful evening gown but a charcoal linen dress with a broad white Thai-silk collar. No flowers in the background, just the Jacobean-print upholstery of the chair, and her red hair simply dressed.

'He's not always sweetness and light, you know, Jo,' Adele offered.

'I had gathered that. Are you comfortable, Mrs Hastings?'

Adele smoothed her skirt. 'I'm fine.' But like a dog to a bone, she returned to her son's ill-humour. 'Sometimes you need to put your foot down with Gavin. I do.'

Jo had started to draw but her pencil hovered suddenly. Why would Gavin's mother feel there was any need for Jo to be putting her foot down? Did she know about her son's intentions?

'Actually, I'm about to put my foot down myself,' Adele continued. 'Over Rosie's schooling. You do know how much I love Rosie, don't you, Jo?'

Jo relaxed. 'Of course.'

'Do you know how long I've been widowed?'

The apparent non sequitur took Jo by surprise, and she shook her head.

'Twelve years. I was very young when I had Gavin and Sharon,' Adele said. 'I'm only fifty-eight now. That's not very old and I've been alone a long time.'

An inkling of where all this was heading hit Jo suddenly. 'Have you…met someone, Mrs Hastings?'

Adele sat forward eagerly. 'Yes, I have. Oh, what a relief to say it! And the thing is, we've really clicked. He's a couple of years younger but still of my generation and—he's asked me to marry him. That's probably why I've been so forgetful lately! I don't know if I'm on my head or my heels—but he lives in Brisbane, you see.'

'Ah,' Jo said, although her pencil had started to fly. 'Hence the problem with Rosie's schooling?'

'Well, I could never abandon Rosie, not after losing her mother like that, but also because I love her so much. But James would be perfectly happy to have her live with us during the school terms. Indeed, he knows that's the only way he's going to get me!'

Adele tossed her head and Jo reached for a crayon as everything she'd been so desperately trying to capture about Gavin's mother, her very spirit, was suddenly all there for her to transmit to paper.

'Uh—Gavin doesn't like the idea of Rosie going away to school?' she suggested.

'He doesn't really. Not yet, anyway. Not that he knows why *I'm* so keen now. And of course I understand his reservations—he adores Rosie. But, well, I could get her into my old school which just happens to be one of the finest. And *I* would be there for her as I always have in the past.'

'So you haven't told Gavin about the man who wants to marry you? Is there any reason not to?'

Adele's blue eyes flashed. 'He's liable to make all sorts of objections.'

'Why?'

Adele hesitated. 'To put it bluntly, well, there's no other way to put it really—I'm a very wealthy woman in my own right, Jo.'

Jo drew in long, flowing strokes, then tiny delicate ones. 'He's afraid you could be targeted by a fortune hunter?'

'Precisely. Anyone would think I came down with the last shower!'

'Rosie does love it here,' Jo murmured.

Adele's shoulders slumped. 'I know.'

Jo glanced at her keenly.

'Of course,' Adele looked indescribably sad for a moment, 'my dearest wish is for Gavin to find someone himself—and a mother for Rosie. He has so much to offer a girl.'

'Provided she can put her foot down,' Jo suggested, and they both laughed.

But as Jo bent her head she didn't see the completely serious look Adele bestowed on her.

Then Gavin's mother said, 'Still, I keep trying. The

people I've invited for dinner tonight have a gorgeous daughter. She's been overseas for a few years. Gavin knows her but he might find her somewhat changed and—who knows?'

Jo's busy fingers stilled at last as she looked up at Adele. 'You're trying to matchmake?'

'Of course. Why shouldn't I? And Sarah Knightly could be just the one to appeal to him.'

Jo blinked, then looked down again.

If that doesn't put the cat amongst the pigeons, Adele Hastings thought, I'd be most surprised. Really, why do young people imagine you're blind and deaf once you reach a certain age? Oh, yes, I'm trying to matchmake, Jo, but it's *you* I'm aiming at for Gavin!

Jo thought seriously about making an excuse not to attend the dinner party.

She told herself she had no desire to witness what his mother might consider suitable wife material for Gavin. She told herself that she might think she was in love with him, but there was also an obstinate little streak in her at war with allowing him to get his own way too often.

She went in the end because some crazy little voice prompted her to think that she'd never seen him in the company of what might be termed a suitable wife, and perhaps she should?

When she went to some lengths to mix and match her limited wardrobe so that she was wearing something a bit different, honesty compelled her to admit she was on her mettle. It made her feel a little forlorn, although she couldn't be sure why.

In the event, she was introduced to Sarah Knightly

and her parents wearing slim taupe trousers and an ivory linen tunic-style blouse. She'd washed her hair and left it loose after blow-drying it, so that it rippled and shone in a silky golden cloud.

She rarely wore make-up but tonight she'd applied eye shadow, mascara and lip gloss.

Her first reaction to Sarah Knightly was—oh, great! One of those tiny, delicate girls destined to make me feel overgrown!

Not only that, Sarah was charming, bubbly but surprisingly mature as she reminisced on her years overseas studying water management in drought-and-flood-prone environments—the last thing Jo would have suspected her of. Her parents, also wool growers, were obviously as proud as Punch of their daughter. Their daughter, on the other hand, was not above batting her eyelashes at Gavin.

As one delicious course followed another—pumpkin soup swirled with cream; tiny, tasty whiting fillets; a magnificent leg of ham, glazed and decorated with pineapple rings and cherries, and a mocha soufflé—Jo counted up all the ways Sarah would benefit Gavin Hastings and Kin Can.

They could discuss in detail, for example, artesian basins and their management. They could do the same with dam placement and how to maximize water runoff. Certainly, Sarah could take her place in any society, not only with her looks and style, but her intelligence. What did that leave?

Rosie, Jo thought, and had to acknowledge that the little girl seemed to be on the back roads of her mind a lot. Of course, she also spent a lot of time *with* Rosie so that would account for it—or did it? Did the fact that she had been motherless herself have anything to do with the growing rapport with, and the affection she felt for, Rosie Hastings?

'Penny for 'em?'

Jo turned to find Gavin at her side, offering her a liqueur. They'd removed to the garden room for their coffee.

'I was thinking,' she said slowly, and took the tiny glass. 'Thank you—I was thinking that Sarah would make a very suitable wife for you.' Sarah was outside, inspecting the pool and garden with her parents and Adele.

His gaze was cool as it flickered over her. 'I see. We're still at war over something, are we, Jo?'

'You started it.'

'No,' he contradicted. 'You started it and are waging it in a veil of silence. That was never my intention.'

Jo stared at him.

'You have to admit you've been avoiding me, Jo.'

Had she? Perhaps, but with the intention of taking the long view rather than being overwhelmed by his physical presence?

'I—' She thought for a moment. 'I'm not avoiding some of the issues now, am I?'

He glanced over his shoulder towards the pool, and frowned. 'You seriously see Sarah as an issue? I don't want her, Jo. Or any of the "suitable wives" my mother keeps parading in front of me.'

Jo blinked. 'You know?'

'Of course I know,' he said impatiently. 'I wasn't born yesterday.'

'I could be forgiven for thinking I was a convenient

wife, Gavin. Not that I'm taking issue with that as such, but since you are going for suitable, you could find someone more suitable—is what I'm saying.' She smiled briefly.

'She got up your nose,' Gavin stated after a long moment.

Jo grimaced. 'Petite girls do sometimes. They make me feel like an Amazon.'

'I tend to feel somewhat clumsy around very petite girls, myself.'

She raised an eyebrow at him.

He smiled, curiously gently. 'Which is why I like you just the way you are.'

Their gazes locked and her heart started to beat slowly and heavily as something flowed between them that was warm and quite lovely.

Her lips parted but he put his hand over hers. 'Later, Jo.'

'Yes,' she agreed huskily.

But no sooner had the Knightlys left than a call came through with the news that a fire had broken out in one of the staff cottages several miles away from the homestead.

'You can't go, Gavin!' Adele protested. 'Your arm—'

'Yes, I can, I must, but only to direct operations.' He grinned. 'You know how good I am at that.'

'Can we help, though? Or, can I help?' Jo asked.

His gaze softened. 'Thanks, but there are plenty of hands, it's direction that might be lacking and it is my responsibility. Go to bed, girls. I'll see you in the morning.' He paused. 'Jo—'

'It's OK,' she murmured.

He hesitated, then turned away.

'He's just like his father,' Adele commented, when he was out of earshot. 'You know you can rely on him!'

It was a while before Jo went to bed.

Something inside her was spinning again beneath that lovely moment of closeness with Gavin Hastings, and she knew that the time was coming when she would be pressed for a decision. She also knew that she very much wanted to marry him. She might get annoyed with his high-handed ways but the burden of loving him was...

She paused her thoughts and wondered why she saw it as a burden when he could make her feel dizzy with delight. When he was the first man to actually do that for her...

When just knowing him made her spin like a top and crave his company. And when the life on Kin Can appealed not only to her artistic senses, but her practical, get-out-and-do-things nature, not to mention her longing for a real home.

Then there was Rosie. She could honestly say that they'd 'clicked'. They spent hours drawing together and Rosie showed some genuine talent. Not only that, they laughed together and Jo had become a confidante.

How *would* Rosie cope with being transplanted from an environment she loved for chunks of the year, and how would she cope with having to share her grandmother with a new husband?

Come to that, what kind of a burden would a six-year-old child put on Adele's new-found happiness, however much Adele might insist she and Rosie were inseparable?

If nothing else, it added up to a lot of good reasons for Gavin to want to marry her, but something was holding her back—the burden of being the one deeply in love while he was not?

'In a nutshell, Jo,' she murmured. 'All your life you've lost the people who meant the most to you. Remember how you felt when you discovered you had a grandmother who'd spent nearly all your life searching for you, but she was gone too? Could this not be a recipe for the same thing if Gavin were to fall wildly, deeply, madly in love again?'

Who is to say he won't fall madly in love with you, Jo? she asked herself.

Then out of the blue something popped into her mind. Was there any form of protection she could take into a marriage of convenience—that was what it was on his side at least—such as not letting him know how much in love she was with him until, if ever, she was confident he felt the same about her?

But then she couldn't help wondering how a sort of 'hedging your bets' policy would affect a relationship. And how hard it might be not to let him see how he affected her. Obviously, she would have to practise some kind of restraint...

The next day brought a sequence of events that seemed to prove to her it was an excellent idea to hedge her bets.

CHAPTER EIGHT

JO WAS sketching in her bedroom, for the first time rather happy with Adele's portrait, when Mrs Harper came to seek her out mid-morning to inform her that Gavin would like to see her, if she was free.

Jo blinked, a little surprised that he hadn't come to look for her himself. She hadn't seen him since the previous evening so she gathered he must have had an early breakfast and gone straight out, and that had also surprised her after what had happened between them last night. But Adele had passed on the news that, although no one had been injured in the fire, the cottage had burnt to the ground, so she'd assumed he was still caught up in the consequences of the fire.

'He's down at the shearing shed. He rang a moment ago,' Mrs Harper added and hesitated.

'Oh!' Jo got up. 'That explains it.' She paused and looked at the housekeeper, who, in turn, was looking troubled. 'It doesn't? Explain it, I mean.'

Mrs Harper opened her mouth, closed it, then said, 'It's not a very nice day, Miss Lucas. There's a perishing westerly blowing; I'd wrap up if I were you. The weather sometimes does that out here. You think it's summer, then winter sneaks in a last left hook.'

Jo took her advice and changed into a tracksuit and her anorak, although she had to wonder why she was being summoned to the shearing shed on an unpleasant day.

In the event, as she jogged down to the shed she found the wind quite exhilarating. There were clouds scudding across the sky and several old peppercorn trees in a clump were tossing their feathery leaves dementedly. Her cheeks were pink; her hair was whipped into a gold tangle as she climbed to the shearing platform.

The shed was swept and empty, except for Gavin who was inspecting one of the electric combs, and she paused for a moment, thinking that he looked rather forbidding.

'Is something wrong?' she asked as she came up to him.

He dropped the comb so that it dangled from its lead and turned to her, and simply regarded her as she steadied her breathing from her run and attempted to tame her hair.

'Gavin?'

'Jo, we need to make a decision,' he said abruptly. 'We've been shilly-shallying around for long enough.'

'Shilly-shallying!' she said incredulously. 'This could be the rest of our lives we're talking about!'

'It's certainly my intention that it is, but we're getting nowhere like this.' He rubbed his jaw moodily, and although he wore clean jeans and a fine, this-time-mulberry wool sweater, he reminded her rather forcibly of the tough man who had taken her hostage.

'Why…what…has something come up I don't know about?' she asked disjointedly. 'Last night—'

'Last night,' he said precisely, 'I was unaware of my mother's intention to remarry.'

'What's that got to do—?' She broke off. 'Of course—Rosie.'

'Yes, Rosie,' he said. 'If she thinks I'm going to entrust Rosie to a man I've never met, who could be some bloody gold-digger anyway, she's mistaken.'

Jo suddenly recalled Mrs Harper's troubled demeanour and made the deduction that, unlike herself, the housekeeper had been within earshot of 'words' at least, between Gavin and his mother.

But her next reaction was incredulity. 'Surely you don't believe your mother would fall for a gold-digger! Don't you think you should at least give her credit for—'

'What?' He glared at her. 'Do you know where she met him? On a cruise. Have you any idea what rich pickings cruises provide for anyone on the make? Rich, lonely widows—'

'Gavin, just stop right there for a moment,' Jo ordered. 'Believe me, it doesn't become you to harbour such scepticism about your own mother!'

'On the contrary,' he drawled, 'it's because I'm extremely fond of my mother, but a realist at the same time, that I'm so concerned.'

Jo took a couple of calming breaths.

'However,' he went on before she could speak, 'even if she marries him and he proves to be OK, there's no way Rosie is going to be involved.'

'Yes, well,' Jo conceded, 'that had crossed my mind.'

'You know about all this?' he shot at her.

Jo nodded. 'She told me yesterday during her sitting.'

'So?'

Jo stopped combing her hair with her fingers and brushed it behind her ears. 'So—what?' she enquired with hauteur.

'Oh, come on, Jo,' he said roughly, 'don't beat about the bush! How did it affect these *prolonged* deliberations of yours?'

'*You* suggested we take some time to think it through!' she cried.

'As I told you yesterday, not like this, in a veil of secrecy and silence.'

Jo discovered in that moment that you could love and hate a man in the same breath. Fair enough, she reasoned, he'd obviously had a shock. Yes, he was obviously very fond of his mother, and she now had a pretty good idea of the wealth involved that would make a lonely widow extremely vulnerable to a man on the make. But this reaction was intolerable even given the circumstances.

'One of my *prolonged* deliberations,' she parodied coolly, 'tells me that a young governess might solve—all our problems.'

'Oh, yes?' he said dangerously. 'How about the fact that we only have to look at each other sometimes to be set alight with need and hunger? Would you prefer to go to your grave wondering about us, Jo? Are you going to play safe all your life? You know,' he said softly, 'I wouldn't have taken you for a coward, not after the way we met.'

She swallowed a lump in her throat and felt dizzy beneath the rush of emotions that came to her as he stared into her eyes. Not like this, something within her cried, it shouldn't happen like this. Not with us both angry but—is he right?

Or—would I be right to hedge my bets after all, at least against the times he can be impossible if nothing else?

She moistened her lips and cleared her throat. 'It so happens I have made a decision, Gavin. I've decided you'd be a very convenient husband for me.'

His eyes narrowed and he made an abrupt movement.

'Let me explain,' she said quietly. 'Of course, there's convenience on both sides. You need a mother for Rosie and that's fine with me. I think we have a special rapport, perhaps because she's motherless and I know what that's like.' She paused.

'Go on.'

It was impossible to tell from his voice or his stance how he was taking it.

'Uh—I've always wanted a home of my own. I guess being a foster-child does that to you, so that's another plus. And, to be honest, I'd have the financial security to draw what I liked. There's a vast range of subjects that appeal to me right here. Kids, animals, landscape.' She looked around. 'Even this old shearing shed.'

His gaze remained narrowed and intent.

'I never did,' she went on, 'intend to spend my artistic career doing commissioned portraits. I saw it as a way to get my work noticed and, once that happened, I always meant to give it away. If I married you, I could give it away a lot earlier. If we agree to this, though, there's one stipulation I need to make.'

'What's that?'

This time there was a detectable response, an echo of harshness in his voice.

She swallowed and took a moment to compose herself. 'That what is past is past and we don't pretend this is anything *but* a marriage of convenience. I know why a "deeply, madly" love match is out of the question for you. You know that I'm something of an independent loner and I'd find it hard to change. But there would be definite advantages for me—as well as you.'

'Does this all lead you to seeing yourself going to bed with me, Jo?'

Her lips parted.

'I mean to say, you sound so damn clinical, we could be discussing the price of eggs.'

'Gavin,' she said through her teeth, 'since the moment you set eyes on me this morning you've been angry and going out of your way to insult me. You're only lucky I haven't slapped your face!'

Her eyes blazed and as she said it she knew that nothing would give her more satisfaction than to do just that—but he saw it coming and ducked, then caught her wrist.

'Whoa,' he said softly. 'Has it occurred to you we're both under a lot of pressure because, rather than adding up the pluses and the minuses, we'd prefer to be doing this—which might just speak for itself anyway.'

She was far too angry to acquiesce when he pulled her into his arms; she was stiff and furious.

'Reminds me—' his lips twisted '—of another time I had you in my arms and you thought you were hating it. In the hut.'

'I was! I am now.'

'Then let me see how I can redeem myself. Will

you marry me, Jo Lucas, not only because of what we can do for each other, but so that we can share a bed, and each other's company, in unity?'

She stared up at him.

'It would be an honour if you said yes,' he added.

She searched his eyes, but could only find a serious query in them. 'Do you accept what I said, though?'

He shrugged. 'If you want me to. I still like to think we care about each other, Jo. I know *I* do and I don't think it would work otherwise.'

Her anger drained away and it was an almost unbearably poignant moment between them. Two people marked and scarred by life—was that enough to hold them together?

It didn't seem to matter to her suddenly. The truth was, she cared so much she couldn't help herself.

She freed a hand and touched her fingers to his cheek, and the assault on her senses was electric. 'OK,' she said huskily.

He heaved a sigh of relief and buried his head in her hair.

Two weeks later, Adele said to Jo, 'You look simply beautiful, my dear!'

Jo glanced down at her wedding outfit, a slim, long, ivory skirt in Thai silk and a short jacket top intricately trimmed with ribbon and lace. Silk covered pumps and short white gloves went with the outfit and a bouquet of yellow rosebuds, just opening, lay on the bed.

Her hair was up and, instead of a veil, a froth of ribbon secured it. Adele had just secured a string of what looked like priceless pearls around her neck, her wedding present.

Rosie, her flower girl, was being dressed by her aunt Sharon in an adjoining bedroom of Gavin's home on the Gold Coast.

The house was also the venue for their wedding. Jo, Adele and Rosie had arrived that morning from Kin Can, to be met by Sharon. Her husband, Roger, Gavin's best man, had Gavin in his keeping in Brisbane.

The house was majestic with sweeping gardens that overlooked an arm of the Coomera River, along which, during the day, a fascinating variety of yachts and boats of all description had sailed in and out from the Gold Coast Broadwater. It also had its own jetty on the river, and a trim, fast-looking craft was tied up to it.

True to tradition, Jo hadn't seen Gavin since the day before.

That might have been why she suddenly sat down on the bed feeling pale and a little ill. The ceremony was due to start in half an hour.

'I feel rather overwhelmed,' she confessed. 'All this—' she gestured to take in the house '—plus, I wanted to do it much more simply.' She stared down at the dazzling diamond on her ring finger.

Adele drew up a chair. 'Why?'

Jo glanced at her, then away. 'I don't know. Second marriage, for Gavin anyway, perhaps.'

'Jo, you're not having second thoughts, are you?'

Jo hesitated.

'Look—' Adele sat forward '—I know it's all been a bit of a rush and I have no doubt you got the third degree from Sharon, she's like that, but I couldn't be happier about this union. I think you're perfect for Gavin and—' she paused '—whatever reservations you may have about it being a second marriage for him, if you love him as I think you do, it will be fine.'

Jo raised her eyes to Adele. 'You know it's a bit one-sided?'

Adele smiled wisely. 'Is it? It looks to me as if he couldn't wait to get you to the altar. Just be yourself, Jo, which in my estimation is a pretty fine person.'

Jo half smiled. 'Thank you.' She stood up and took a deep breath. 'I'm ready.'

It was a lovely wedding. Everyone thought the bride looked stunning, and there was no doubt that the groom was enough to take your breath away in a dark dinner suit with a blinding white shirt front—he took the bride's breath away, anyway.

Rosie was adorable in a long yellow dress with flowers in her hair, and highly excited—she still couldn't quite believe her luck: a mother! And one she liked very much.

Adele was the epitome of elegance in a lavender lace gown and even the groom's sister dabbed her eyes as Jo and Gavin were pronounced man and wife.

Jo had formed the opinion that Sharon Pritchard née Hastings had all of her brother's 'born to command' qualities with little of his charisma, but she couldn't doubt Sharon's affection for Gavin.

There were about thirty people at the reception in the flower-decked dining room that flowed out to the garden. Case and Mrs Harper attended. So did Jo's flatmate and best friend, Leanne, and a few more friends. Her favourite art teacher was there.

On Gavin's side, it was mostly family, cousins, uncles and aunts, but he'd also invited some of his married friends, and laughingly told them—thank heavens, no more ghastly blind dates!

Adele, in a spirit of mischief, Jo could only assume, had invited Elspeth Morgan and her husband.

Of course, Jo detected some surprise and speculation as Gavin made sure he introduced her to everyone. You couldn't deny it was a rushed wedding; you couldn't deny that most of them had never heard of her until the invitations had arrived.

Two of his aunts had studied her midriff area quite blatantly, then withdrawn to have a cosy chat. One of his uncles had asked Jo if she was a Mount Miriam Lucas. Before she could reply that she wasn't, he'd gone on to congratulate Gavin on making a damn fine connection.

'You'll get used to my family,' Gavin said into her ear at this stage. 'We're a weird mob.'

'What's so good about a Mount Miriam connection?' she whispered back.

'Old, very old money.'

'I'm sorry! I did tell you you could do better for yourself,' she reminded him with a smile lurking at the backs of her eyes.

'Jo—' But they were interrupted and he never got to say it.

One thing did impress itself upon her during her wedding reception. The Mount Miriam connection might be about old, very old money, but the Hastings connection wasn't so far off that mark either.

Of course she'd known it was quite an empire Gavin had inherited, but for the first time she got a real glimpse of the upper echelon, rather rarefied society she'd married into. Some of them might be quirky, but all the Hastingses had one thing in common: the confidence that came from 'old money'.

Then it was over. Instead of her and Gavin leaving, the guests left, including Rosie, who was going to stay with her Pritchard cousins for a few days. Jo didn't change but she threw her bouquet and pale blue garter—Rosie caught the bouquet—and then they were alone, apart from the catering company discreetly clearing away.

'Tell me something,' Gavin said as he led her into a glass-fronted terrace that overlooked the river. 'Do you feel really married to me now?'

Jo looked around. The terrace, the whole house, had a Tuscan feel to it. There were citrus trees and miniature Cyprus trees in tubs on terracotta tiles, there were wooden planter boxes growing a riot of impatiens in every colour; there was a fountain with underwater lights looking like drowned stars.

She turned back to him and said after a moment's hesitation, 'I certainly feel very publicly married to you.'

'Good.' He strolled forward with his hands shoved into his trouser pockets. 'That's what I intended to achieve.'

Jo raised an eyebrow. 'Why?'

He stopped in front of her and studied the exquisite outfit, the gold of her hair, her creamy, flawless skin and the grey of her eyes as well as the pulse beating rapidly at the base of her throat. 'So you, and every-one else, would know it's for real.'

'You thought there might be some doubt?'

'None whatsoever on my part,' he answered obliquely, and studied her carefully again. 'May I make a suggestion? Gorgeous as you look, let's change, and relax out here for a while.'

'Good idea.' She glinted him a little smile, then looked down at herself and touched the pearls. 'I haven't given you my present yet. I'll get it at the same time.'

'Off you go, then. I'm going to organize a bottle of champagne since you had a glass and a half at the most earlier.'

'It seemed like a good idea to stay sober.' She laughed.

All her things had been moved into the master bed-room, she discovered, and she raised her eyebrows as she closed the door and looked around.

Someone—Adele?—had gone to town, here. What looked like acres of fawn carpet, a wide bed beneath a bedspread of unbleached cotton ecru with an intri-cate self-pattern, and heaped with scatter pillows cov-ered in fawn wild silk with pearl beadings.

Behind the bed stood a beautiful folding screen that immediately caught her attention—birds of paradise painted on a mushroom foil background.

At the other end of the room two linen-covered armchairs were set around a coffee-table and there was a magnificent elephant wonderfully carved from green verdite, ears extended, trunk raised, one foot bent on its plinth as if it were striding across the veld. It stood about waist-high.

She walked across to it and stroked the smooth green and brown mottled stone. 'Jambo, jumbo! I like you very much!'

Everything had been unpacked for her, including the wedding present Adele had insisted on giving her—a trousseau. She'd turned a deaf ear to Jo's protests on the matter although she had allowed Jo some say in choice of garments.

Amongst them was a pair of silky apricot long trousers with an elasticated waist, wide legs and a matching loose blouse. Jo chose them and changed into them after one last look at herself in her wedding outfit. She took the ribbons out of her hair and brushed it until it gleamed. She left her pearls on and looked around for her present for Gavin.

It was on a bedside table, beautifully wrapped. She picked it up and hugged it to herself and took several deep breaths.

The time was coming and coming fast when she might have to explain something that Gavin didn't know about her...

The time was also coming when she might discover how she matched up to his first wife.

He was waiting for her, not changed, but without his jacket and tie, with his shirt sleeves rolled up and his collar open.

On the low table in front of a deep, comfortable settee stood a bottle of champagne in a stone cooler, two glasses and a tray of snacks.

'You didn't eat much either,' he said as she eyed the snacks.

Jo fingered her rings—the diamond now had a gold band behind it—and wondered what he'd say if she told him nerves had seen her have difficulty swallowing? Then she remembered she had his present tucked under her arm.

'This is for you,' she said a little awkwardly. 'I hope you like it.' She held it out to him.

'Thank you.' He eased the gold ribbon off and opened the wrapping, and went quite still for a long moment. It was an exquisitely framed oval portrait of Rosie, looking over her shoulder with all the vivacity that made her such a character.

He looked up at last. 'Oh, Jo, you've captured her to a T.'

'It did feel as if it was going well,' she said huskily.

'Thank you,' he said simply.

He put the portrait down and came over to her, taking her chin in his hand. 'Missed me?'

'I...why?'

'You look a little shell-shocked and a bundle of nerves all rolled into one. I wondered if being torn from my side yesterday until you walked down the aisle today had anything to do with it?'

She grimaced. 'I did have a moment of sheer panic,' she conceded.

His eyes narrowed. 'Oh?'

'Your mother talked me out of it.'

'How?'

'She told me just to be myself,' Jo said after a slight hesitation.

He frowned, then shrugged. 'I had my own moment of panic.'

Jo looked up into his eyes. 'You wondered if we're doing the right thing?' she hazarded.

'Not at all. I was afraid that's what *you'd* be wondering.'

Jo blew her fringe up and smiled faintly. 'It's done now. There's just one thing—' She paused, then frowned and turned towards the river as shouts and screams floated across the water, then there was a burst of flame and a loud bang. 'What on earth…?'

Gavin reacted swiftly. 'A boat on fire.' He strode towards the terrace doors. 'Stay there, Jo, I'll—'

'No way!' she protested as, by the light of the fire, she saw people leaping from the burning boat into the water. 'Just let me do this.' She took her pearls and engagement ring off, laid them on the coffee table and ran after him.

Next to the sleek cruiser tied to Gavin's jetty was an inflatable dinghy with an outboard motor. 'We've got to take the tide into consideration,' he said as they climbed aboard. 'It's going out so it should carry the boat towards that mangrove island.' He gestured towards an uninhabited island opposite. 'But it could also carry anyone in the water the same way. Jo, I wish you'd stayed behind!'

He pulled the starter chord of the outboard and it roared to life.

'I can help pull people out of the water,' she shouted over the motor.

'Yes, but, although one fuel tank has exploded, there could be others.'

'Just—there, Gavin.' She pointed at a head bobbing in the water.

They spent the next hour rescuing swimmers, and several non-swimmers, two of whom Jo had to dive in and rescue, and depositing them on the jetty. They were joined, thankfully, by other dinghies from houses along the river and several Coastguard and Air Sea Rescue boats with fire-fighting equipment aboard.

As Gavin had predicted the burning hulk ended up in amongst the mangroves across the river, and a second fuel tank did blow up, showering burning debris into the water, but fortunately no one was struck.

All the same both she and Gavin were wet, filthy and exhausted by the time the rescue operation was complete, and after being interviewed by the Coastguard, they staggered back to the terrace room, took one look at each other and collapsed onto a wooden bench laughing feebly.

'Here.' He got up and poured them a glass of champagne. 'It'll be flat and warm by now, but we deserve it.'

Jo sipped hers. 'Tastes wonderful.' She glanced down at herself. 'How on earth are we going to get clean without dripping mud and heaven knows what all over the carpets, et cetera?'

'Hmm...well, not a problem.' He walked over to the fountain, or so Jo thought, but he stopped at a panel beside it and opened a door set in the woodwork to reveal a switchboard. At the touch of several buttons, one end of the terrace room was transformed.

Blinds descended blocking the view to the river. What had appeared to her to be a circle of parquet wood tiles on the floor split down the middle and each half of the circle slid back to reveal a spa bath. Underwater lights came on in the spa and it started to bubble.

The last thing he did was switch all the other lighting off except the drowned stars in the fountain.

Jo put down her glass and clapped spontaneously. 'Your mother?'

'My mother,' he agreed. 'Neither the architect, the engineer, nor the electrician and the plumber she badgered into producing this have ever been the same since. She got the idea from a Japanese bathhouse.'

'But it's masterly!' Jo laughed. 'I can't wait to get in and get clean.'

'Be my guest.' He touched another panel and a door swung open to reveal a cupboard of terry towelling robes, bath towels and cakes of handmade soap, loofahs, even long-handled back scrubbers.

Jo pulled her ruined clothes off and stepped into the water in her bra and knickers, still laughing delightedly.

'I would say that,' he commented, 'to get the full benefit one would need to be naked.'

'Naked it is, then,' she conceded cheerfully and, beneath the cover of the foaming, bubbling water, removed her underwear. 'Could you please pass me the soap?'

He did so, plus refilling their glasses and finally stripping to his underpants and joining her.

'Thank heavens no one was killed—thank you.' She took her glass and lay back with a luxurious sigh. 'It could have been a whole lot worse.'

'It could have. And you were exceedingly brave, Jo.'

'Not really. I'm a strong swimmer but—' she paused, then glinted a wicked glance at him '—we make a good team. We could even go into business together.'

'We do—it struck me once before. A sort of Tarzan/Jane partnership?' he suggested.

Her laughter bubbled up again and she sipped her champagne, then put it down and began to soap her arms.

'Actually, I have a better idea,' he said. He took the soap from her. 'Now that is what I had in mind.' And he began to soap her.

'I see what you mean,' she murmured after a while as she lay still beneath his wandering hands, and felt her tired, over-exerted body relax, then come alive to other sensations. 'That's lovely.'

'So are you.' His mouth closed on hers.

It started out slow and languorous, the way he kissed her and held her with their bodies feeling weightless in the water as they blended together. A gentle union after the preceding high drama. A lovely let-down still riding on their friendship and the way they'd worked together so well.

Then the tempo changed as his fingers moved more and more intimately on her until she found herself sitting across his lap with his face in her hands as she kissed him and acknowledged that she was being seduced out of her mind—and loving every moment of it.

'Jo—' he breathed and ran his hands down her back to cup her bottom, '—come with me.'

'In a minute.' She went back to kissing him.

'Jo, now. We need a bed.'

She opened her eyes and looked into his to find they were dark with desire—urgent need, in fact. 'OK.'

She put her hands on his shoulders and raised herself off his lap. He groaned and, despite his urgent need, held her waist and kissed her dripping breasts.

'I thought you said—'

'I did, we do, my lovely wife. Let's go.'

They got out, grabbed two robes and shrugged into them, then, holding hands, ran through the house to the master bedroom.

Had it ever been treated so cavalierly? Jo wondered, as wild silk, pearl-trimmed scatter pillows were thrown aside and the ecru bedspread summarily dispatched to the floor with two white robes thrown on top of it.

As for her 'hedging her bets' policy that had included practising restraint so that he would never know how much she wanted him, talk about throwing it out of the proverbial window!

But she couldn't help herself. She was on fire in a way she'd never thought she would be. She needed his lean, strong body; she needed everything about Gavin Hastings to be her very own, to make her whole, to love her...

'Jo?'

'Gavin?'

They stared at each other across the bed. 'Have I ever told you how lovely you are?' His gaze flickered down her body.

'Yes, but I don't mind how often you do it,' she replied gravely. 'Have I ever told you that you're rather gorgeous?'

'You once told me I was pretty.'

She grinned. 'If you lie down on this bed, I'll amend that.'

'Done!'

In fact they lay down together and quite soon their laughing moment became something else.. red-hot desire but, this time, he took the lead until she was helpless with longing and mindless with rapture.

'Now, Jo?'

'Yes, please,' she gasped.

'Good. I'm just about to die.'

'*You're*—I thought I was.'

'It must be mutual, then.'

It was.

It was also quite some time before they spoke again. By that time they were lying side by side, their heads close on the pillow.

He said softly, 'Wow!' Then he stroked her cheek.

Jo slid her fingers through his, and blew her fringe up. 'Make that a double wow!'

He sat up, but only to pull a sheet over them. 'Of course I always knew it had to be like that.'

'How could you possibly?' She turned to look into his eyes.

He pushed her hair behind her ear. 'There was something about the way you tried to pulverize my toes when we first met that must have alerted me,' he said thoughtfully.

She hid a smile. 'You know what I think?'

'Tell me.'

'You're an impossible know-all, Gavin Hastings.'

'On the contrary, Joanne Hastings—' he caressed her body beneath the sheet '—I'm a very good judge of—character.' He curved his hand possessively around her waist.

'Character?'

'You know what I mean.'

She was laughing helplessly. 'I do know what you mean but I feel it has another name.'

'So you—um—were prey to it right from the beginning?' he queried. 'This thing by another name?'

'To my horror and complete confusion, yes.' She grimaced as she recalled their first few hours together.

He laughed and kissed her. 'Shall we sleep?'

'I think it would be a good idea. I'm bushed,' she confided. 'Not everyone has such an eventful wedding day.'

'Indeed. Comfortable?'

'Yes,' she answered drowsily, and a few moments later she was asleep.

Gavin Hastings watched her for a while, and found himself recalling the minutes before they'd been alerted to the fire on the boat.

What had she said? Something about—*it's done now*.

Hardly an acknowledgement that it had been the right thing to do, getting married, he mused, and wondered why those three words lay like a prickle on the surface of his mind.

Of course, the greater mystery was why she'd elected not to tell him she was a virgin. Or was that what she'd been about to say? *There's just one thing*…hadn't those been her words?

The thing was, he hadn't expected it. She was so cool and confident most of the time, she *was* twenty-four, and even though she'd told him she didn't enjoy being kissed, he'd assumed she wasn't completely in-experienced even if they hadn't been particularly successful experiences.

So what was in her background to account for it? And how serious had she been about insisting this was a marriage of convenience? Nothing that had happened between them tonight had been 'convenient'. There was a basic mutual attraction that was extremely powerful, although, on the other hand, he thought dryly, she'd gone out of her way to keep him at arm's length for the preceding weeks.

He studied her in the lamplight. Her gold hair was gorgeously mussed. Her creamy skin was still flushed and warm. Her mouth— Damn it, he thought, why did she have to have the most kissable mouth he'd ever seen? So that he was almost unbearably tempted to kiss her awake and take her again…

His thoughts ranged back over the evening. She was right—in any kind of a crisis they made a good team, but he'd been trained for it. Yes, he'd always had good reflexes, good co-ordination to start with, but she was also a natural with all the above plus steady nerves. He had to admire that and it made them two of a kind, but…

But what? he wondered. Why do I get the feeling there's a girl within this girl I might never be allowed to know—and that it's going to bug me, and go on bugging me until I do find the real Jo Lucas?

CHAPTER NINE

THEY had five days on their own.

Dreamy, peaceful days for the most part when they swam and went boating, talked, read—and made love.

They had some electrifying encounters when their need for each other got quite out of hand...

He took her out to dinner one night. She dressed carefully in a simple, sleeveless black dress with a square neckline, against which her pearls looked fabulous. She put her hair up, and knew immediately as he narrowed his eyes briefly that he didn't approve. But she was rather pleased with it so she left it as it was. Her finishing touch was to spray some perfume behind her ears.

'Ready?' He was lounging in the doorway wearing navy trousers and a cream linen shirt.

She slipped on her high-heeled sandals. 'Ready!'

They ate on the waterfront at Sanctuary Cove, a resort complex with wonderful shops, a marina and a great variety of restaurants. Jo loved it, and before they sat down they strolled through the village, with its ornate lampposts and flower-decked pavements, window-shopping. Then they walked down one of the marina arms admiring the boats.

And she was really enjoying her dinner when, suddenly, Gavin pushed his Lobster Mornay away and announced that he couldn't do it.

'Do what?' She stared at him with her knife and fork poised.

'Eat.'

She frowned. 'Why not? Mine's lovely.'

'It should be down, not up.'

'How could—' Her grey gaze was mystified as she inspected his plate. 'Are you talking about the lobster?'

He shook his head. 'Your hair.'

Jo expelled an exasperated little breath. She'd forgotten all about that disapproving little glint in his eyes as she'd tied her hair up in a knot. 'I'll take it down when we get home.'

'Why not now?'

She glanced around. 'Don't be silly, Gavin. It— that would be—' she sought the right word '—unhygienic.'

He sat back and fingered his jaw. 'Isn't it clean?'

'It's perfectly clean,' she countered with a touch of asperity. 'You saw me wash it earlier.'

'So?'

She eyed him. He looked *perfectly* relaxed with the line of his shoulders wide and comfortable under the cream linen, but just the thought of them did strange things to her.

As an artist she found the perfection of those broad shoulders and his sleek, muscled torso were an invitation she now knew she couldn't resist transmitting to paper.

As a woman and a lover she knew they were a source of desire and joy and the thought of being in his arms and his bed made her feel weak at the knees—but now, here? Surely he couldn't stir her up in that rapturous way in such a public spot?

'Jo?' He said it softly and watched that delicious pulse beating rapidly at the base of her throat.

'Um…well, it's not a good idea to spread even clean hairs around at the table,' she said a little raggedly.

'I'm not asking you to wave it about, just let it down, slowly and carefully, if you like. Actually, slowly and carefully would be best. For me.'

That's just like asking me to undress slowly and carefully for you—it shot through her mind. And some colour spread up her throat to her cheeks. 'It's not good manners, Gavin.'

'Then we better go home—' he stood up and held his hand out to her '—since good manners mean so much to you.'

'I haven't finished,' she protested.

'I could take it down for you.'

'My hair? No! Not here!'

His lips twisted. 'My point entirely. Come, Josie.'

People were already starting to look at them oddly.

'I…we can't just walk out. You haven't paid or anything.'

He gestured dismissively. 'They know me.'

Jo looked around into what appeared to her to be dozens of pairs of amused, quizzical eyes. She put her napkin on the table hurriedly and stood up.

She also said, through her teeth, 'Does that mean you make a habit of this?'

'No. You're the first woman to do it to me.'

Their gazes locked and there was something unsmiling but electrifying about the way his eyes lingered on her.

So much so she turned on her heel and walked out ahead of him with her head held high but every secret, sensual spot beneath her skin clamouring for his touch.

The ride home was fast and they didn't talk at all. He didn't bother with putting the car in the garage, but pulled up outside the portico, and spun the wheels on the gravel of the drive.

They only just got inside the heavily carved front door before he put a hand on her shoulder, saying grimly, 'Do you know you've been driving me crazy for the last two hours with that stern, prim, bloody knot?'

'Oh?' She examined her mixture of annoyance and intrigue—intrigue that she could drive him crazy simply by tying up her hair. Even so, she reminded herself, he had embarrassed her so the big question was—how to deal with such conflicting emotions?

Something dealt with it for her. Something she couldn't name within her told her that two could play this game.

'How about this, then?' she murmured, and slipped off her shoes. The hall tiles were cool beneath her feet.

She looked around and took her pearls off and hung them from one of the hands of the bronze Hindu goddess who presided over the hall. Then she reached for her zip and her black dress floated down her body and pooled at her feet. She stepped out of it gravely, picked it up and hung it over the other of the goddess's hands.

Then she attended to her hair and, when it was released, shook her head so that it swirled in a gold cloud, and she put her hands on her hips. At the same time she noted how heavily he was breathing as he studied the fascinating play of a delicate black lace bra and hipster briefs on the creamy satin of her skin.

'No Bonds Cottontails tonight,' he said.

'No.'

He looked into her eyes. 'Am I allowed to touch?'

'No-o.' Her voice cracked a little but her gaze was firm. 'Not until you apologize.'

'For what?'

'Embarrassing the life out of me.'

He raised a satanic eyebrow. 'You don't see it as a compliment?'

'I may eventually. Right now—well, would you like me to be honest?'

'Be my guest,' he rasped.

Jo considered for a moment and examined her sudden sense of unreality, even unease. 'I'm far more interested in solving this rather savage state of affairs between us.'

A glint of something different entered his eyes. 'How?'

'I don't know. In the meantime, I'm going to bed.' She turned and walked away from him.

She didn't get very far. He came up behind and put his arms around her. 'Like hell you are without me if that's what you had in mind, Jo Lucas,' he growled into her ear and brought his hands up to cup her breasts. 'OK, I'm sorry, but I couldn't help myself.'

She hesitated.

'Let me show you,' he murmured, and moved his

hands down her waist to slide them beneath the top of her panties.

She caught her bottom lip between her teeth. 'That's…' She couldn't go on as she grew warm and wet with desire.

'Am I forgiven?' he breathed against the side of her neck.

She leant back against him. 'I'm tending towards being more complimented,' she said slowly.

'Good.' He turned her round and swept her up in his arms. 'Let's see if I can compliment you further.'

'These,' he said later, 'also drive me mad.'

They were lying on their sides, facing each other. Once again the wild silk pillows were scattered around the floor and the coverlet lay in a crumpled heap beneath his clothes and her bra and pants.

He pushed himself up on his elbow and stroked the curve of her hip.

Jo stretched her arms upwards and pointed her toes. 'I'd never thought about them particularly.'

'Well, if I suddenly ask you, in the middle of dinner, to get up and walk away from me, you'll know why.'

Her breathing jolted. 'I see that I'm in for some exciting times.'

'Mmm. Like right now.'

From the word go, it became extremely sultry as he kissed her from head to toe and revelled in the perfume of her skin, her secret, most intimate spots. And as she gave herself up to the ever-growing excitement, she made her own explorations of his hard, honed body until there was only one place to go.

They went down that road together in perfect unison, holding, tasting, touching and thrilling each other with the sensations they aroused as never before.

And when it was over they lay exhausted in each other's arms, and fell asleep in a tangle of sweat-dewed limbs.

'Jo?'

Her lashes fluttered up to reveal daylight filtering through the curtains, then she turned her head to see Gavin watching her with a frown in his eyes.

'Yes?' She struggled to sit up. 'Is something wrong?'

'Are you all right?'

'Of course. Why?'

He groaned and buried his head between her breasts for a moment. 'I don't know what got into me last night.'

She subsided and her mouth curved. 'Neither do I—I mean, I don't know what got into me. Oh, no.' She sat up again with her hand to her mouth.

'What?'

Although there was no live-in staff, a middle-aged housekeeper, who went by the name of Sophie, came in daily.

'My dress. My pearls!'

Instant understanding came to his eyes. 'You feel Sophie might get the socks shocked off her to find them hanging up in the hall?'

'Yes! Would you…would you be a darling and get them for me?'

'Too late. I heard her come in by the front door about ten minutes ago.'

Jo looked stricken, so much so, he had to laugh. 'She's a married lady with four children and two grandchildren.'

'She may have forgotten what it can be like, in that case,' Jo replied gloomily.

'What it can be like,' he repeated with a reminiscent smile and pulled her back into his arms. 'I haven't. But rest assured she's too well paid to make you feel uncomfortable about it.'

Jo relaxed against him. 'What if she gossips?'

'She's too well paid for that also, and she signed a confidentiality clause anyway.'

'Do you really have to go to those lengths to protect your privacy, Gavin?'

'Uh-huh. As a matter of fact I've stepped up our security since the kidnap attempt. Everyone we employ is now fully vetted first, not only household staff.'

'I always did get the feeling the Kin Can connection was on a par with the Mount Miriam one,' she teased.

Strangely, a variation of that subject, in the form of other problems great wealth could attract, came up a few days later when their official honeymoon was over.

They were still on the Gold Coast but the embargo Gavin had placed on any business—even phone calls—had been lifted, and Sharon Pritchard came down for a visit with her three girls as well as Adele and Rosie.

They had a fun lunch, then Gavin took the kids for a spin in the speedboat leaving Sharon, Adele and Jo to pore over the wedding photos Adele had brought with her.

'Just look at her,' Adele trilled as she pointed to Elspeth Morgan, captured talking very earnestly to one of Gavin's uncles, the same one who had assumed Jo was a Mount Miriam Lucas.

'She was wasting her time if she was trying to impress Uncle Garth,' Sharon said with a chuckle. 'He's as mad as a hatter and ''new money'' doesn't appeal to him in the slightest.'

Adele agreed but added the rider, 'Mind you, there's an awful *lot* of Morgan money and I guess it's not that long ago that we were all new money.'

Sharon waved a languid hand. 'At least we know the dynasty is secure again. Or *can* be, heaven-willing.'

'Sharon,' Adele reproved.

'Secure?' Jo questioned, suddenly looking up from a photo of her and Gavin. 'In what way?'

'In the way of you having sons, darling,' Sharon said succinctly. 'Gavin looked all set to be the first in a direct line of Hastings not to have a male heir, which was a bit of a worry. Nor have I helped exactly by having three daughters.'

Jo turned to Adele with a frown in her eyes.

'Take no notice, Jo,' Adele commanded. 'That's all nonsense. Sharon—' she turned to her daughter '—you can be as bad as Elspeth Morgan! Things don't work that way these days.'

Sharon grimaced. 'Maybe, but you can't deny it would be a huge burden for Rosie's shoulders. And you can't deny that a girl can be very much at the mercy of the man she marries.'

Jo swallowed and looked down at the photo in her hands. She and Gavin were standing side by side looking into each other's eyes and her first glance at the photo had produced a little thrill. Now, all she could think was, amongst his admitted need of a wife, had he neglected to tell her he needed a son?

And was the rest of the Hastings family thinking along those lines? Two of his aunts had certainly had it in mind at the wedding, she recalled.

'Sons can be just as capable of squandering an empire as sons-in-law not brought up to it,' Adele observed prosaically.

'Well, I can't help thinking you showed such a brave, steady, practical nature throughout that ghastly kidnapping business, Jo, that your genes added to Gavin's would produce fine sons.' Sharon reached for another photo.

Jo, Gavin and Rosie waved Adele, Sharon and her girls off later that afternoon.

'OK, catfish,' Gavin said to Rosie, 'we've got two more days down here, then it's back to Kin Can. How would you like to spend the time?'

'I would *love* to go to Sea World! They have some polar bears there. I saw them when they were babies. Have you seen them, Jo?' Rosie turned to her excitedly.

'No.'

'Sea World it is tomorrow, then,' Gavin said. 'Anything else?'

'No, I'll just enjoy being with you two. I wanted to ask you something, Jo. Should I call you Jo or Mum?'

For some reason Jo glanced across at Gavin over Rosie's head and she saw him narrow his eyes suddenly.

'Oh, I think Jo is fine, Rosie, don't you?' she said after the barest hesitation. 'For the time being anyway.'

'What would you *like* to call her, Rosie?' Gavin intervened.

Rosie drew a deep breath. 'You know how we said goodbye to my mother before the wedding, Daddy?'

'Yes, sweetheart,' he said quietly.

'Well, although I never knew her, she was my real mother and I was worried that it wouldn't be right to call someone else Mum, although I'm thrilled to have a new mother,' she assured Jo earnestly. 'Does that make sense?' she added anxiously.

'Perfect sense,' Jo said softly. 'That's fine with me, Rosie.'

'What about,' Gavin said out of the blue as they were getting ready for bed that night, 'our other kids?'

Jo had wrapped herself in a cotton robe and was sitting brushing her hair at the dressing table. She looked up at his reflection in the mirror and she felt her nerves tighten as she recalled his sister's thoughts on dynasties.

'What about them?'

'We do plan to have a family, don't we, Jo?' He came up behind her and took the brush from her. He hadn't changed yet and he wore jeans and a navy T-shirt.

'We didn't discuss that.'

He'd started to brush her hair but he stopped

abruptly. 'I sort of assumed it went without saying.' His eyes in the mirror were intent and probing.

Jo swallowed. 'So did I, I guess. Although perhaps not immediately.' She frowned. 'Are you saying that I should have encouraged Rosie to call me Mum?'

'I'm just wondering if it won't make her feel a little on the outside if she's the only one not to.'

A fleeting smile curved Jo's lips. 'How many do we plan to have, Gavin?'

'It's up to you.' He resumed brushing.

'Look,' Jo said slowly, 'to be honest, I was feeling my way with Rosie. And you,' she added and shrugged. 'It's a delicate area for both of you—as she proved.'

'You thought I might object to her calling you Mum?'

'Yes, I did. Oh, it would be perfectly natural,' she assured him. 'Your memories—'

'Don't include Rosie calling anyone Mum,' he broke in.

'Gavin—' Jo swung round on the stool and took her brush back '—we seem to be on different wavelengths here. Please tell me exactly what you're thinking.'

He sat down on the end of the bed opposite her. 'I just thought it might be practical—' He stopped and looked down at his shoes. 'The thing is, because of the way it happened, I have no memories of Sasha mothering Rosie. On the other hand I have very clear memories of mentally ranting and railing on how unfair it was that Rosie should have been deprived of a mother.'

'You—somehow or other you took her to say good-bye, though,' Jo said huskily.

'Yes. Sasha is buried in the family graveyard on Kin Can. I thought we both needed to say goodbye.' He looked up suddenly. 'I didn't expect it to hit Rosie that way, however.'

Jo considered it all and found herself feeling as if she'd entered a minefield. For the last five days they'd been so close, she and Gavin, she'd lost sight of what she'd assumed was the underlying reason for this marriage—Rosie.

Then, that very afternoon she'd had the importance of sons thrust at her—and here was Gavin talking about starting a family almost right on cue, however it had come up. Not to mention his concern that Rosie would be melded seamlessly into their family unit.

Naturally she would share that concern, she reflected. On the other hand, why did she have the feeling that the honeymoon was well and truly over and providing sons for the Hastings dynasty was coming at her like a runaway train?

Was she imagining it all? Had it simply been a series of coincidences that the subject should have been touched upon the way it had? Or—was Sharon right in thinking she had been summed up *genetically* and found acceptable? Hadn't they agreed only days ago that they were well matched?

Her gaze focused on Gavin suddenly. Had that been the basis of his conviction that he needed to marry her and her only—not quite as unclear as he'd told her?

And what about the conviction she had right now that he wasn't being completely open with her?

'Jo?'

'Uh…' She made an effort to concentrate. 'So far as Rosie goes, I think it would be wise to take things slowly.'

'How about the rest of our family? Slowly, too?'

'Gavin, we've only been married for six days!'

His lips twisted. 'I know. But it is on your agenda, to have kids?'

She raised the brush and stroked it through her hair. 'Why would you doubt it?' she asked.

'You can be—rather secretive, Jo.'

'In what way?'

'I may be wrong, you're very athletic and active, but I got the feeling you were a virgin.'

'Is that what this is all about?' she asked incredulously. 'You have a grudge about that?'

'Not *per se*. If anything I was—honoured. I just can't quite work out why you didn't tell me.'

'It so happens I was just about to tell you when a boat blew up in the river!'

'And after that?'

'It didn't seem…I mean, I'd planned to tell you because I was afraid I might seem, well, awkward, but that didn't happen, thanks to you.'

His gaze softened.

'Besides,' she added, 'we did agree that what's past is past.'

'So I'm not to be allowed to know why you reached twenty-four without ever having a lover?' he queried.

'No one—' she paused '—measured up to you, Gavin.'

Something sharpened in his eyes. 'Then it wasn't

only convenience you had in mind when you married me, Jo?'

'I never said it was.'

He looked ironic. 'It featured quite prominently, but, anyway—how say you now?'

They stared at each other.

'Why do I have the feeling you've got me in some kind of dock and are pressing charges?' she asked huskily.

'Wouldn't it be natural to examine our feelings now it's—let me rephrase—*it's done now*?'

The words seemed to echo in her mind but she couldn't pinpoint why. And she tried to take hold then, but she couldn't help thinking that her decision to hedge her bets might still be a wise one—until she discovered what this was all about and how desperate he was for a son, at least.

She stood up and walked over to the window, from where she could see the channel markers in the river flashing red and green. In her disturbed state of mind they seemed to mirror her dilemma. Green for 'go for broke' and simply be honest with him? Or, red for extreme caution required, pass this point and you're liable to end up on the rocks?

Rocks such as not being able to produce a son to order, for example?

'No, I don't think it would be wise to get academic at this stage, Gavin,' she said, not turning. 'What we've had so far has been lovely. Let's just go forward and try to build on it.'

He didn't reply for a long time, and then he didn't reply in the spoken word. He came up behind her and put his arms around her, and simply held her until she relaxed against him. Then he started to nuzzle her neck and finally, when she was feeling weak at the knees with desire, he took her to bed.

But although their love-making was intense and wonderful, she couldn't help feeling she'd survived a crisis.

Over the next three months she woke gradually to the realization that she was still living that crisis, and that it might have two names. Not only sons, but memories of Sasha?

CHAPTER TEN

THE weather had warmed up considerably three months after Jo's first arrival on Kin Can. She got up one morning and she dressed in khaki shorts, a pink blouse and slipped on sandals. Gavin had risen before the crack of dawn to supervise a muster.

She reviewed her plans for the day as she and Rosie ate breakfast. They were going to work on the doll's house they were building together. Not that it was a doll's house in anything but concept. Rosie had no time for dolls so this was a miniature shearing shed complete with sheep, since Rosie had adopted an orphan lamb to add to her menagerie of a puppy, a pony and a tame cockatoo.

It was going well, Jo thought suddenly, her elevation to motherhood. Not only that, she was enjoying it. She'd persisted with her plan to take things slowly and not force a motherly presence on Rosie and it was working.

One of her worries had been that Rosie might resent having to share her father with someone else, particularly a wife. It was all very well to yearn for a mother, but at six, and never having had one, all the implications could come as something of a shock, she'd reasoned.

But Rosie had shown hardly any signs of that. She threw herself whole-heartedly into all the things they did together, swimming, drawing, reading, as well as being out and about on the property. She'd begun to consult Jo on what to wear, she'd started to confide in Jo about her friends and Jo's suggestion that they build a miniature sheep shed had been a winner.

On the odd occasion when Jo did detect that Rosie longed for her father's undivided attention, she took herself off to draw, leaving the two of them together, sometimes for a whole day.

Rosie had always been completely restored when she'd returned.

The truth was, she mused, the little girl was twining herself more and more into her heartstrings, and there came, one day, a sign that the same was happening to Rosie—the day they ganged up on Gavin, as he put it.

It started over the orphan lamb. Rosie smuggled it into her bedroom, where it made a considerable mess in the traditional manner of infants, not to mention sheep.

Mrs Harper was so horrified that, despite being a fan of Rosie's, she made mention of the matter to the 'boss'.

The lamb was banished, Rosie was distraught and accused her father of being cruel and horrible. When the fact was pointed out to her that not even her puppy was allowed in the house, she stamped her foot and told Gavin that was cruel and horrible too, and now she really hated him!

Jo went quietly away at this stage and consulted Case. That afternoon a prefabricated enclosure and rather large kennel made its appearance in the garden below Rosie's bedroom.

Jo took both Gavin and Rosie to see it before dinner and she made the suggestion that the lamb and the puppy, on the strict understanding that neither could be let into the house, might cohabit happily in the garden, close to Rosie's room.

Before Gavin had a chance to say yes or no, Rosie flung her arms around Jo and told her, with real affection, she was the best mum a kid could have. Jo hugged her back and discovered that to see Rosie restored gave her a lovely warm feeling.

Gavin, observing all this, said at last, 'I see.'

'What do you see, Daddy?' Rosie trilled. 'Isn't it a smashing idea?'

'I see that the two women in my life have ganged up on me,' he said with unusual solemnity.

Rosie slipped her hand into Jo's. 'But we do love you,' she assured him. 'Can I go and get them now?'

He nodded and his daughter raced off.

Gavin looked into Jo's eyes.

She grimaced. 'Sorry, but…' She shrugged.

He took her hand this time. 'It's going well?' he suggested.

She relaxed. 'It's going well.'

He kissed her. 'You've been wonderful,' he said as he drew away, 'but you do realize that either the puppy is going to grow up thinking it's a sheep or the lamb is going to grow up thinking it's a dog?'

Jo started to laugh.

A few days later, Rosie mentioned that she was looking forward to having babies.

Jo and Mrs Harper exchanged startled glances.

'I don't know about brothers,' Rosie continued.

'My friend Julia's little brother is terribly naughty but I wouldn't mind a sister.'

Both Jo and Mrs Harper hid relieved smiles.

Jo came back to the present and went on reviewing her day. Before she did anything else, she would have her weekly conference with Mrs Harper where they discussed what entertaining was upcoming, what needed to be ordered in and the like. Running such a large establishment was quite complex, Jo had discovered, and she would have been quite happy to leave it all to the super-efficient housekeeper had it not been for Adele.

She'd flown in not long after Jo, Rosie and Gavin had got back from the Gold Coast, when Gavin had to leave again to attend a board meeting in Sydney. And she'd been quite adamant that Jo should learn all the ins and outs of Kin Can from the lady-in-charge's perspective.

Of course the Hastings men liked to think they were the ultimate authority, she'd informed Jo, but much of the responsibility for the smooth running of the place would fall on her, she would find.

During the next few days Jo had had to agree with her and she'd come to admire Adele's touch with the families who lived on the station, the household staff and how she'd gone out of her way to make their lives on a vast sheep station, in the middle of nowhere virtually, as pleasant as possible.

She'd initiated a sewing circle, a book club and she'd started a video library. She suggested to Jo that she might like to give art classes. She'd made it quite clear that Kin Can was a show-piece of the wool industry and needed to be maintained as such for the buyers of wool and rams who came from all over the world to visit.

She'd also impressed upon Jo that even when your neighbours were as far-flung as they were in this part of the world, a sense of community was vital.

'So you see, my dear,' she finished, 'it's important for you to get involved and to put your own stamp on things.' A glint of humour lit her eyes. 'Not only for the good of the station, but you yourself. Otherwise there are times when a sheep station can drive you crazy.'

Jo laughed. 'So far I'm loving it. There's so much space and freedom.'

'Good,' Adele approved. 'Any time you need a helping hand, just give me a call.'

'How—' Jo hesitated '—are your marriage plans going? I was only thinking the other day that I felt a bit guilty about Gavin and I rather overshadowing everything else.'

Adele grimaced. 'I'm having second thoughts.'

'Because of what Gavin might have said to you about—' She broke off a little awkwardly.

'Gold-diggers? Fortune hunters? Lonely widows?' Adele heaved a sigh. 'It's awfully complicated when there's a lot of money involved,' she said sadly. 'But yes, he could be right. I may have got swept off my feet.'

Jo said nothing but pressed Adele's hand warmly. Yet her mother-in-law's sentiment brought back the subject of sons and heirs to her mind.

Not that Gavin had mentioned a family again, but those thoughts had stayed with her as she'd experimented with taking up the reins of being the mistress of Kin Can.

Nor had their physical need for each other diminished. If anything it had broadened as she got more and more involved in the life of the station and was able to share it with him.

But there was something she couldn't put her finger on at first. Something between her and Gavin brought her a fleeting sense of unease, and she found herself examining it again as she sipped her coffee that morning.

So far as hedging her bets went, she didn't think she was. Yes, she hadn't told him she loved him; yes, she still, for some reason she didn't quite understand herself, headed off any talk of her past. But she thought she matched him in bed and out of it.

Except for the odd occasion when she sensed a suppressed frustration about him that reminded her of their conversation over what Rosie should call her. Reminded her, come to that, of his mood the night she'd worn her hair up out to dinner.

The more she thought about it, the more she wondered if it had only been desire between them that had got out of hand. Or was there more to the unsmiling electricity they generated sometimes?

Then she started to wonder if there were ways she was not matching up to Sasha, ways she was unaware of?

Of course, they had been in love, Gavin and Sasha, but what more could he expect of her when he himself had made the comment that the less flamboyant emotions were the ones with better foundations?

They got along so well for the most part, until she

found that chasm opening up at her feet when she least expected it, as had happened to her recently.

A couple of weeks ago he'd flown her to Brisbane ostensibly because he'd had some business there. They'd dropped Rosie off with Adele and he'd checked them into a beautiful hotel on the Brisbane River. He'd told her that he would have to leave her alone for most of the day but she might appreciate the opportunity to shop or whatever. Then he'd requested a dinner date with her.

She'd agreed with suitable gravity and they'd parted, but she'd been filled with a sense of anticipation.

She hadn't shopped, she'd taken the opportunity to visit a new exhibition at the Queensland Art Gallery she'd been dying to see. Then, succumbing to an unusual whim, for her, she'd had a facial and got her hair done.

It had certainly made it even more pleasurable to don one of her trousseau dresses—a lovely cream linen shift—knowing she was also well groomed.

They had dined at a restaurant overlooking the river, and perhaps something in the way he'd been watching her had alerted her, so that she said suddenly, 'Oh no.'

He raised an eyebrow. They'd finished their main course and were deciding whether to have dessert or not. 'Something wrong?'

'Well—' she touched her newly washed and styled hair '—my hair is down, so it can't be that.'

He lay back in his chair looking impossibly attractive in a dark suit, a pale blue shirt and a navy tie.

'You're not going to ask me to get up and walk away from you?' she queried.

He sat up. 'I wish you hadn't said that.'

She stayed sober with an effort. 'Something tells me it might not be a good idea to have dessert, though.'

'Your instincts are impeccable, Jo.'

She could no longer hide a smile. 'I must be learning.'

It wasn't far from the restaurant to the hotel, and once in their room, he set about undressing her leisurely.

When there was nothing left to take off, he said quietly but with palpable restraint, 'Now you can walk away.'

Jo thought for a moment. Was this turning into another of those unsmiling encounters between them that disturbed her for all their electricity?

'I think I'd rather help you undress first,' she countered. 'We need some—equity, don't we?'

But was she asking a different question? she wondered. Or making a statement along the lines of—we need to be together in spirit, Gavin, not just physically.

'You always did have a mind of your own, Josie,' he said after a long pause.

'Mmm,' she agreed, and put her hands on his shirt buttons.

There was nothing leisurely about the way Gavin got undressed, and there was nothing leisurely about the way they made love. It was urgent and powerful and their climax was mind-blowing...

'You kill me, you know,' he said into her hair, when they were capable of talking again.

Jo moved cautiously in his arms. 'If it's any consolation I feel as if I've been dropped from a great height.'

He lifted his head and looked into her eyes, with his entirely wicked. 'But it was nice?'

'It was…' she sighed luxuriously '…fantastic.'

'When…?' He stopped and his eyes changed.

'When what?'

'No, nothing. Go to sleep, Lady Longlegs.'

'Gavin—' she hesitated '—tell me what's on your mind.'

'Not a lot.' He reached out and switched off the bedside lamp.

Jo opened her mouth to protest that she could sense a definite change in him, a withdrawal, and she needed to know why.

But it occurred to her suddenly that maybe he was remembering Sasha. Maybe they'd done unexpected little trips like this—perhaps they'd stayed in this very hotel, and it was his memories he was fighting.

If so, there was nothing she could do or say.

He stayed mentally withdrawn from her until they got back to Kin Can, then, as had happened before between them, they got back to normal.

But there was also the day she'd hosted her first dinner party. She flinched at the memory.

She'd invited three couples, all from the district, and it had been going really well until one of the men, under the influence of too much wine, had raised his glass to Gavin and complimented him on the fact that he sure knew how to pick his wives.

A horrified silence had greeted his words. The man's wife had looked as if a handy hole in the ground was her preferred option, and Gavin had shot him a murderous glance.

Somehow, Jo had found the composure to get the evening going again but not with the same level of enjoyment as before and she'd been sincerely relieved when it had been over.

'Remind me not to invite him again,' she murmured to Gavin as they waved their guests off for their long drives home.

'Why? He obviously approved of you.'

She blinked, then turned to him incredulously. 'If nothing else it was the height of tactlessness,' she objected.

He shrugged and turned away. 'I think I'll turn in.'

Jo stayed on the veranda for some time, trying to work out how she'd been made to feel as if she'd invited the comment. That's crazy, she told herself angrily. Or had one highly tactless comment brought Sasha back for Gavin? Sasha, presiding over dinner parties as only she could, perhaps?

Sasha, whose shadow I'm beginning to feel more and more, she thought. Nothing else seems to make sense. On the other hand, he *told* me in so many words he would always be holding another woman up to her memory, so why am I surprised and so hurt?

She went to bed, to find him fast asleep—the first time since their marriage he hadn't reached for her, even if only to hold her in his arms until they fell asleep.

She put her coffee-cup down now and sighed at

those difficult memories. Then she forced herself to contemplate the rest of her day.

Once her session with Rosie was over, she intended to sneak a few hours' drawing. She was building up a series of pictures of the station, and was seriously thinking of giving an exhibition. Adele, who seemed to know anyone who was anyone, had also got interested in the project.

But her afternoon session didn't happen. She ended up going to bed with a hot-water bottle.

She did eventually fall asleep, and although the worst was over when she woke up she felt drained and pale. Gavin was sitting on the side of the bed.

'That time of the month?' he queried, and put his hand over hers.

'Mmm.' But as she agreed she couldn't help wondering if it was a flash of disappointment she saw in his eyes.

'You stay there and relax. I'll bring some supper later.' He bent down and kissed her gently.

She drifted off to sleep again, convinced she'd imagined the disappointment. In fact, at that moment she felt cherished and as if she could forget all her previous concerns. That they were all right.

The next morning she was up and about and back to normal. But she was quite unprepared for the conversation she had with Gavin while they took a break for morning tea, or 'smoko' as everyone on the property called it.

They'd ridden their bikes to one of the lambing paddocks. Rosie had been flown to a neighbouring property for a birthday party and was to stay overnight.

Jo had been delighted with the lambs, then she'd spread a blanket under a tree and unpacked the basket Mrs Harper had provided. There was tea in a Thermos flask and some slices of rich, dark fruit cake bursting with cherries.

'I could get fat on Mrs Harper's cooking,' she commented.

Gavin sprawled out across the rug as she poured the tea into enamel mugs. 'You don't look fat to me.'

'Thank you, Mr Hastings. You should know,' she teased.

He studied her comprehensively in jeans and a checked blouse, then looked into her eyes. 'Are you still happy with the way we "know" each other, Jo?'

She hesitated and frowned—another unsmiling moment coming up? 'The way we know each other is fine with me,' she said carefully. 'How about you?'

'Ditto,' he said. 'Incidentally, is there anything you can do for what you seem to go through every month?'

Jo selected a piece of cake and handed him the plate. 'Go on the pill or have a baby,' she said humorously.

'Does that mean you aren't on the pill?'

She set her mug down carefully on the lid of the cake tin and waved away some flies. 'What made you think I was?'

'It's been three months,' he pointed out.

Jo shook her head to clear her thoughts. 'And you're worried I'm infertile after only three months? Or secretly taking the pill?' she asked.

'You did say you didn't want to start a family immediately, Jo.'

It struck her that she hadn't imagined that look of disappointment in his eyes the previous evening, after all. And her fears, all her insecurities bubbled up again in a way that was suddenly impossible to resist.

'And you neglected to tell me, Gavin Hastings—' she got to her feet abruptly '—what this marriage really was about! A son to carry on your line.'

'Nonsense,' he replied roughly and stood up himself. 'What gave you that idea?' he added contemptuously.

'The idea came from several sources, actually. You've just confirmed it.' Her eyes flashed and she planted her hands on her hips, but inside she was feeling cold and incredibly hurt. Here I go again, she thought. Having my motivation mistrusted when— talk about motivation!—his has always been suspect.

'You did stipulate this was very much a marriage of convenience, Jo,' he pointed out lethally, as if reading her mind. 'Convenient in the sense that you can walk away from it whenever you feel like it? Is that what you meant?'

Her lips parted to deny it, but she changed her mind. 'I never intended it to become a child-bearing operation to save the Hastings dynasty.'

'So you aren't planning to have a family?' he shot back.

'Not to order, not like that, no! Incidentally, if I don't provide you with a son, Gavin, will I get my marching orders?'

He crossed the gap between them swiftly and grabbed her wrist in a bruising grasp. 'Stop it,' he ordered through his teeth. 'That has nothing to do with it as you damn well know!'

'No, I don't *know*. Let me go, you're hurting me,' she gasped.

He dropped her wrist, but his expression was still infuriated and menacing. 'Jo—'

She turned on her heel and ran to her bike, evidently taking him by surprise because she was able to switch it on and drive away from him before he could stop her.

And she drove with her hair streaming out behind her, a blur in front of her eyes as tears and a dreadful ache in her heart claimed her.

She just didn't see the kangaroo that bounded out from behind a clump of rocks until she hit it and cartwheeled over the handlebars.

The kangaroo picked itself up and bounded off. She lay unconscious on the ground.

'Gavin,' Tom Watson said, 'I think she's going to be all right. She's sprained an ankle, she has an impressive array of grazes, but I don't believe there are any internal injuries or skull fractures—a bloody miracle, actually. I'm going to fly her to Charleville for more tests all the same.'

'When do you expect her to regain consciousness?'

Tom regarded him for a moment. He'd known Gavin Hastings for a long time but he'd only ever seen him look like this once before, when his first wife had died. 'Hard to say. You better come with us.'

'Yes, you go, Gavin,' Mrs Harper said tearfully as

she bent over Jo's inert form on a stretcher, and patted her shoulder tenderly. 'I'll take care of Rosie when she comes back.'

'Where am I?'

Jo's lashes fluttered up and Gavin immediately pressed the bell beside her bed.

'You're in hospital, Jo, but you're going to be fine.' he said quietly, picking up her hand. 'You had an accident on a quad bike—do you remember?'

'No-o.'

Tom came into the room and drew up a chair beside the bed. And patiently and gently he asked her some questions. It took a while but they eventually established that she knew who she was, she knew who Gavin was—although that brought a frown to her eyes—and the only thing she didn't remember at all was the accident.

The effort of it all obviously exhausted her and she fell asleep.

Tom drew Gavin out of the room. 'That's quite common,' he said. 'Some people never remember the actual incident, but otherwise I'd say her memory hasn't been affected at all.'

He paused and searched Gavin's eyes for signs of relief. But his expression was as hard and shuttered as it had been all through the long day and half a night.

'Gavin? She's going to be all right, believe me, mate. Look, I know what this must be bringing back memories of, but—'

'The thing is,' Gavin broke in swiftly and harshly, 'do you know how I'm ever going to be able to forgive myself?' And he turned and strode away down the corridor.

Tom stared after him, then shook his head and went back to his patient.

A couple of days later, Jo felt a lot more coherent although, at the same time, as if she'd been under a steamroller, and she was still being treated for concussion.

Then Tom came to see her and, while he examined her, he took a light, playful approach.

'Don't know what it is with you two,' he said. 'If you're not getting yourself shot by kidnappers, you're getting knocked out by kangaroos!'

Jo smiled weakly, but after Tom's departure she found herself considering his words with a feeling of irony. What was it between them that had seen them end up in the same hospital, same private ward, at the beginning and quite possibly the end of their relationship?

Although she still didn't remember running into the kangaroo, the events that had led up to it had slowly filtered back.

So how ironic was it, she reflected, that from this very bed Gavin became possessed of the impulse to marry her, and her alone? How—fateful—that she should be in it, not really broken in body but certainly in spirit, because there'd been times when she'd thought—what? That she was winning his love and he hadn't married her only for Rosie and sons to carry on the line?

Five days after the accident, Jo was dressed and ready to leave hospital.

She still felt, although it was lessening, as if she'd

been under a steamroller. She still had bruises and grazes, but her ankle had responded well and she could put her weight on it. Otherwise she was fine.

She grimaced at the thought. She certainly wasn't fine mentally.

Gavin had spent quite a bit of time with her, but had said nothing about the argument that had led to the accident. He'd been gentle and determinedly cheerful. At first, while she'd felt so sick and sore, she'd been grateful, but today she felt different. In about half an hour, he was coming to fly her back to Kin Can. So they could formally dissolve their marriage? she wondered.

Was that what she wanted? What were her options? To continue in the knowledge that her principal role in his life was as the mother of his children? No...but...

She gazed out of the window. It had rained almost the entire time she'd been in hospital and was still raining.

Gavin stood at the door of Jo's private ward and watched her narrowly without her being aware of it.

Her lovely hair was tied back in a pony-tail and the lines of her figure beneath a black T-shirt and loose grey cotton trousers were tense and upright as she sat on the side of the bed half turned towards the window.

What was she thinking? he wondered. Was she still as angry with him as she'd been five days ago? Was she contemplating leaving him?

She was pale, he realized, from the one cheek he

could see, and there was still a bruise on it. Her hands were gripped in her lap as if she was in pain. He closed his eyes briefly and cursed himself yet again.

Then he took hold. 'Jo?'

She swung round convulsively, her eyes widening. 'I...I didn't hear you,' she stammered.

'I haven't been here long. How do you feel?'

'Fine! Fine.' She gazed at him with, he got the odd feeling, expectation.

'Shall we go, then? I've had a slight change—'

'Gavin, we need to talk! I need to know where we stand.'

'This isn't,' he said quietly, 'the time or the place. Anyway, you can't be all that fine yet and it's best that we just take things slowly for a time.' He glanced out of the window and grimaced.

'I'm perfectly able to talk,' she said tautly. 'I—I'm not a porcelain doll, but that's what you're making me feel like!'

'Jo, we could have a slightly difficult trip ahead of us so let's talk when we get home.' He picked up her bag.

She stared at the angles and lines of his face and his shuttered expression, and trembled inwardly. How could they have come to this? He might make her feel like a porcelain doll, but she knew she was banging her head against a brick wall at the moment.

CHAPTER ELEVEN

IT WAS one of the station Range Rovers Gavin led Jo to, and he said, 'Sorry about this, but we're driving.'

She looked surprised.

'Things have got tricky overnight. There's been a lot of flooding and the plane was seconded to fly a pregnant woman to Brisbane. Nor is there one damn chopper in the district that isn't on search and rescue missions. But I've put an extra sheepskin over the seat to make it more comfortable.'

'Thanks.' Jo climbed in. 'How are things out at Kin Can?' she added as he got into the driver's seat.

He switched on and drove out of the hospital car park. 'Wet. We've still got access in and out but we're having to move sheep up to higher ground.'

'That bad?'

'Uh-huh.' He flicked on the radio. 'I was tempted to leave you in hospital for a day or so but they need all the beds they can get. There've been some real emergencies with the floods.'

'I didn't realize it was so bad,' she said with a tinge of guilt.

He flicked her a glance. 'No. Well, you did have other things on your mind.'

Jo gazed at her hands. 'Gavin—'

But he stilled her with an upraised hand, then pointed to the radio.

It was a road and weather report being broadcast,

and he swore fluently. 'The main road is cut. We'll have to go the long way round.'

'Perhaps we should go back to Charleville?'

He grimaced. 'There's not a spare bed for love nor money in Charleville and the Warrego is rising fast so Charleville may not be so safe itself. Don't worry, I'll get you through.'

It was six horses stranded in a flooded paddock that caused their downfall.

Jo noticed them first. 'We can't just leave them,' she said.

He hesitated, glancing at her stricken expression. 'No.' He pulled the Range Rover up beside a huge gum tree. 'I'll have to open up the fence. Stay where you are,' he ordered.

But without wire-cutters it was easier said than done to open up the barbed-wire fence so the horses could reach the relative safety of the higher ground beside the road. And Jo couldn't believe how swiftly the water was rising.

In the end she ignored his order and got out to help him. It was pouring now out of a low, sullen, steel-grey sky as he used the tools from the Range Rover's toolbox to unwind the wire from a corner post.

'They shouldn't have horses in barbed-wire pad-docks in the first place,' he said bitterly at one stage.

'Here.' She'd gone to the vehicle and brought back some of her clothes to wrap around his hands that were scratched and bleeding.

'Thanks. Nearly done.'

'Where will they go, though?' she questioned anx-iously.

'Back down the road if they've got any sense—and

they do have great survival instincts when they're not fenced in, plus they're strong swimmers,' he said, breathing heavily. 'Can't believe I'm sweating when I'm so damn wet. There.' He unwrapped the last strand and the fence was open.

In a flurry of hooves and flying manes and tails, the horses galloped out of the paddock, and as he'd predicted, took the road back to Charleville.

'Thanks, it was nice of you to help us but got to go!' he said with some irony and Jo grinned.

But he sobered rapidly as they got back into the car. Water was already lapping the side of the road. 'That little ''good Samaritan'' act may have cost us, Jo. Let's get the latest info.'

It wasn't good. The flood waters in their immediate vicinity were rising rapidly, both in front of them and behind them.

He switched off the car radio and clenched his fists. 'I must be out of my mind. We won't get through now.'

'You couldn't have just let them drown,' she said shakily.

'It might come down to them or us. Listen, I'm going to check in on the CB radio, and then I'm going to investigate that tree.'

He used the CB radio, talking tersely into it and getting patched through to the SES, State Emergency Services, and one of their helicopters, giving them their position and their situation. Then he moved the Range Rover into position right beside the tree.

'Oh, good heavens!' Jo breathed as she stared out of the window. There was a wall of brown frothy water crossing the paddock towards them.

'Just do exactly as I say, Jo,' he commanded. 'I'll help you up onto the roof.'

If that was a painful experience for her, what was to follow was worse. Gavin managed to throw a tow rope over the lowest branch of the tree and he climbed the tree like a big cat.

'It's quite solid, quite safe, Jo,' he called down to her as he tied the rope onto the branch, then lowered one end down to her with a loop on it. 'Now put the loop over you and around your waist, and I want you to come up exactly as I did.'

'But it's so smooth, I don't think I can!'

'Use all the little knobs and knots you can find for your feet. Don't worry if you slip, I've got you and I can help hoist you as well.'

She hesitated, but the water was up lapping against the car doors now. She put her hands on the tree and felt the rope tighten around her waist. And slowly, agonizingly slowly, somehow she began to inch her way up it.

He talked to her all the time, but as she was just out of reach, with her lungs bursting, she froze and knew she could go no further.

'Jo, grab my hand!'

She looked up to see him lying along the branch with his hand held down to her.

'I can't,' she gasped, clinging to the tree trunk. 'I can't reach.'

'Yes, you can. Jo, I *love* you. I've loved you since that very first day.'

'*What?*'

'I wasn't going to tell you until later, when we got home, but it's true. Just another few inches, Jo.'

'But you've been so...so...'

'I told you I was a bad loser!'

'I know you can't forget her, Gavin—'

'It's you I'm petrified of losing. Please, my darling, just a few more inches. We can do it!'

She did it. She never knew how she achieved it physically, except to know that without his strength and his SAS expertise she wouldn't have made it. But, perhaps, what he'd said had been the most powerful impetus of all, and just as the Range Rover started to float away she was huddled into the crook of the tree, breathing like a train, and he was sitting astride the branch in front of her.

'What did you say?' she panted.

He touched her face. 'I love you, sweetheart. I've been going quietly insane for the last three months wondering when, if ever, you were going to fall in love with me.'

Her lips parted, but before she could say a word they heard a helicopter approaching.

He squinted upwards and then down at the rising flood. 'Thank God—and I mean that. This time you'll have a winch to pull you up, and I'll be with you.'

'Never seen the like of it,' the pilot of the State Emergency Services helicopter yelled over the roar of the rotors. 'If it's any consolation, Gavin, both Charleville and Cunnamulla are on high alert now.'

'How about Kin Can?'

'The news isn't good, I'm afraid.'

'Rosie,' Jo murmured urgently.

'She's in Brisbane.' He held her against him.

'Where are we going?' he asked the pilot.

'Roma. Still dry there, although the Mitchell is rising too. But I'm afraid that's as far as I can take you. I need to refuel and get out again—there are dozens of emergencies.'

'Can you take me out to Kin Can?' Gavin shouted.

'Sure, mate, but it's going to be a fast turnaround!'

'Jo,' Gavin said into her ear, 'I'm going to send you down to the Coast from Roma. I need to get back to Kin Can—can you understand?'

'Of course. But be careful. I just couldn't believe how quickly that all happened!' she said dazedly.

'I know—these things have to be seen to be believed—but I will be careful. You too. I can't imagine how you must feel now on top of all your other sore spots.'

'I think I'll be OK.' She nestled into him, then looked into his eyes with a smile in hers. 'You know, I led a very dull but *safe* life until I met you!'

He kissed the tip of her nose and laughed as he marvelled, 'Kidnappers, boats exploding, floods, helicopter rescues—maybe something about our meeting caused the planets to go on a collision course?'

She laughed back, nestled against him again and they didn't talk any more; it was too exhausting making themselves heard.

She had four days in the house on the river before he came back to her.

Thanks to all the confusion due to the floods, Roma's airport had been no place for any further explanations as he'd gone about organizing a flight for her. But he'd cupped her face just before he'd left and said very quietly, 'Tell me you understand?'

'I do.'

'That's my Josie.' He kissed her, then let her go.

Adele had met her in Brisbane and driven her down to the Coast, where there'd been a doctor waiting to examine her, despite her protestations that she was fine.

'Well, you are, Mrs Hastings,' he said finally, 'apart from some new bruises, grazes and strained muscles. I'd take it very easy for a while. You did have concussion, then having to climb a tree to escape a flash-flood—' He shook his head. 'I'm going to leave you a couple of mild sleeping pills.'

Adele took a long look at Jo when the doctor departed, then insisted she do just that. Go to bed and take a sleeping pill.

'I...' Jo started to say, but the truth was she was mentally reeling from all the events of the day, and one event particularly.

'I'll be here,' Adele continued. 'But have a bath first to help wash away any stiffness. Have a spa! Everyone tried to tell me I was insane over that bath but I knew it would come in handy one day!'

Jo opened her mouth to tell her mother-in-law that the spa had already performed one good deed for her, then she decided against it.

And it did help, so did the sleeping pill, although she woke very early and lay very still as she pictured Kin Can under water—and the miracle and mystery of what Gavin had said.

Did I imagine it? she wondered. Was I hallucinating from sheer strain? Did he say it only to get me to make that vital extra effort? Why can't I altogether believe it?

She stared at the light rimming the curtains as the sun rose and found herself recalling their angry conversation before she'd crashed the quad bike. She remembered how everything had added up to one thing—sons.

She remembered his determination not to talk about their marriage when he'd picked her up from the hospital, and how, so suddenly, that had changed...

She did rest for most of that day, as muscles she hadn't known existed protested at any unwise movement.

Adele insisted on staying with her, saying that Rosie was fine with Sharon and she loved her cousins' company.

But the following day, when Jo was feeling better, she suggested that Adele needn't stay on with her.

They'd just received the news that everyone left on Kin Can was fine except for a lot of it being waterlogged.

'These things happen,' Adele said philosophically. 'Charleville all but disappeared in the last big flood. It's not only the rain in the area, it's the result of monsoon rains in the north. But life in outback Australia was never meant to be easy with its cycles of drought and flood. Uh—no, dear, I'm not going to leave you until Gavin gets back.'

'I'll be fine—' Jo stopped rather abruptly and narrowed her eyes. 'Is this what I think it is?'

Adele grimaced. 'Probably. I've had strict orders to stay with you until he gets here.'

'That's…' Jo breathed rapidly.

'Typical Gavin,' his mother agreed. 'I've also been told to keep Sharon away. Apparently she rather thoughtlessly caused some mayhem between you and Gavin?'

Jo subsided but said nothing.

'On the other hand,' Adele continued after a long moment, 'after what you've been through, Jo, I wouldn't feel good about you being here, or anywhere, on your own. So you're just going to have to make the best of me!'

'It's not that,' Jo protested. 'I thought I might be taking you away from—whatever.'

'Well, you're not,' Adele said comfortably. 'And I have some good news.'

Jo frowned.

'I got a phone call from a friend of mine this morning. She runs an art gallery of some repute. She'd be very interested in holding an exhibition of your work.'

Jo gasped. Then her eyes softened. 'One thing I do know—I couldn't have a better mother-in-law!'

Adele looked set to take issue with the statement, but in the end she held her peace, and said only, 'One thing I *promise*, as soon as Gavin arrives, I'll disappear.'

He came two days later.

It was early evening and Adele had ordered a light, informal meal that they would eat early so Sophie could get away.

It was set out on a table in the terrace room, with a bottle of wine. There were open smoked-salmon sandwiches and tiny quiches; two individual sashimi platters decorated with carrot and onion pickles in a soy and ginger sauce; a heaped bowl of fresh, peeled prawns and Sophie's famous, secret-recipe seafood sauce. There were home-made rolls and, for starters, two lidded bowls of asparagus soup.

Jo, who had several grazed patches of skin on her body that were still healing, had changed into something light and cool—a pair of Miss Saigon wrap-style pyjamas in a dusky pink with plum-coloured blossom embroidery.

She'd just lifted the lid off her soup bowl and was inhaling the lovely aroma, when he walked through to the terrace, taking both Jo and Adele by surprise. They hadn't had any messages from him since the day before.

'Well, what a lovely surprise!' Adele rose. 'I take it things must have improved out west?'

'Yes. It's peaked and subsiding rapidly now. Hi, Jo.'

'Hello!' She put down her linen napkin and stood up herself, and it occurred to her she was drinking his presence in through her pores. She certainly couldn't think of anything else to say.

There was also quite a bit about him to remind her of his bushranger image. His jaw was blue with stubble, his khaki shirt was torn at one elbow, his jeans were stained and his boots were caked with dried mud.

'What's the damage?' Adele asked.

'The only place to escape flooding was the home-stead—' he smiled as his mother heaved a sigh of relief '—but the stock losses were more than I'd hoped for. Still, we did the best we could.'

His gaze returned to Jo, standing beside the table like a frozen statue. Then he looked down at himself ruefully. 'I think I ought to take a shower. I could even smell! This seat on a plane came up unexpectedly so I grabbed it. Will you excuse me for a few minutes?'

'Of course,' she said, coming to life at last. 'We'll organize some more food in the meantime.'

'No need for that, Jo!' Adele objected. 'I'm heading off right now—'

'But you haven't had a bite and—'

'Sharon can feed me,' Adele said blithely. 'And as you know I don't have to pack. All I need is my book, my purse and my car keys.'

This was true. Adele kept three complete sets of clothes and cosmetics. One at Kin Can, one on the Coast and one at her home in Brisbane. She'd also advised Jo to do the same—one of the practices of the rich Jo had found amusing at first, until she'd discovered it saved an awful lot of time and preparation.

'Well—'

'Now, you take care of yourself, my dear!' Adele came over and kissed her warmly. 'You too, mate!' She saluted her son, and was gone.

Leaving Jo and Gavin staring at each other with Jo, unknowingly, reflecting all her fears and uncertainties in her eyes.

He moved abruptly, then looked down at his grimy hands. 'Give me five,' he murmured and turned away.

Jo sat down again, and covered her soup. The sun

had set and there was just a lingering soft gold light over the river and the mangroves. But for once in her life, she didn't respond mentally to the colours and shapes before her eyes as she wondered what was to come. For, with each succeeding day away from him, her awful fear that there was some catch to what he'd said had grown.

'Jo?'

She turned to see him standing beside the table in clean khaki shorts. His hair was wet, his beard was still in place and he was pulling down a yellow T-shirt. If he smelt of anything it was soap and clean clothes.

'Uh—that was quick.'

'Mmm,' he agreed and fingered his jaw. 'Sorry about this but I get the feeling I've been away for far too long as it is.'

He picked up the wine and poured two glasses. 'You look as if you could do with it.'

'Thank you.' She accepted the glass and their fingers touched briefly.

He sat down and raked his hand through his hair, scattering droplets. 'What's the problem, Jo?'

She opened and closed her mouth several times, then, 'I...when I thought about it, it didn't seem to make sense.'

'I never—' he captured her gaze '—gave sons a second thought when I asked you to marry me.'

She blinked incredulously. 'You said...I can't help knowing that starting a family is a primary concern of yours,' she stammered.

'Because of some guff Sharon spouted about dynasties? If you're wondering, I got that bit of information out of my mother.'

'It didn't help,' she conceded, and took a sip of wine. 'But it wasn't only Sharon. You yourself led me to believe it.'

'Yes, it was a primary concern,' he agreed. 'But it had nothing to do with sons or dynasties. It seemed to me to be the one way I'd get to keep you.'

Her lips parted. 'You didn't think—I don't understand.'

'I didn't either.' He paused and grimaced. 'I guess it didn't seem possible for me to have fallen madly in love in a matter of hours. Of course I'd also sworn off "deeply, wildly, madly" but not, I now know, for the reasons I told you when we were handcuffed together.'

'No?' Her voice was threadbare as different emotions claimed her. Seeds of hope?

'No. Because what Sasha did for me wasn't to ruin me for any other woman, as I thought. She taught me what the real thing was, and it was a wonderful legacy she gave me. I was just too blind and stupid to see it. But what she did leave me with—was a deep fear that I could lose someone I loved, as I lost her.

'As the months passed,' he went on, 'it all became clear to me—from my point of view anyway. But you—' he smiled, although with no amusement '—stayed the same lovely enigma you'd always been.'

She closed her eyes briefly.

'And I couldn't help wondering if, when our marriage was no longer convenient, you would simply move on. That's why I wanted to start a family, so you wouldn't be able to.'

They stared at each other.

'That's why,' he added quietly, 'I could never tell you how I felt—until I was afraid I was going to lose you to a flood. I couldn't bear the thought of hearing you say it hadn't happened for you.'

'So—' she cleared her throat '—you hedged your bets by not letting me know how you felt?'

'Yes. I'm sorry.'

'So did I.'

There was a little silence as he regarded his glass, then looked across at her with a frown. 'What do you mean?'

'I mean that I fell in love with you when you first asked me to marry you—and then you passed out cold. It just—' she moistened her lips '—it just came like that.'

He stared at her incredulously.

'To be honest,' she said with a shaky little smile, 'I didn't ever think I was hiding it that well.'

'Jo,' he said hoarsely, 'why hide it anyway?'

'It was such a miracle for me, I couldn't bear to think it was so…so one-sided. And I reasoned that if you didn't know how I felt it would be—I don't know—like a form of self-protection.'

'I guess I can understand that all too well,' he replied slowly and with a trace of grimness. 'But why was it such a miracle?'

She sighed suddenly. 'I lost everyone I'd *ever* loved, my parents, my grandmother. My father's mother, who looked for me nearly all my life then died before I was found. It makes you scared—'

'I know that, sweetheart,' he interrupted, 'from my own experience. And you have no idea how often I told myself not to forget *why* you might be such a dedicated loner. It was getting harder to convince myself, though.'

'There was another reason. I swore once never to depend on anyone, and it's the real reason, I guess, why I didn't think I would ever fall in love.'

She took another sip of wine, then told him factually and unemotionally about what had happened to her at fifteen.

'Oh, Jo,' he said softly and with such a wealth of understanding and concern as he covered her hand with his, sudden tears beaded her lashes.

'The thing is,' she said, 'you swept all that away almost as if it had never existed.'

'I did?'

She nodded.

'Almost?' His fingers tightened on hers.

'It came back to hit me when you told me you thought I might be secretly on the pill. Not the revulsion, but the memory of not being *believed* in. That's why I got so angry and felt so hurt. That's why I did something so stupid like running into a kangaroo.'

He got up and came round to draw her to her feet. 'I *love* you, Jo Lucas,' he said intently. 'Deeply, wildly and madly. Will you marry me?'

Her grey eyes widened. 'We are married.'

'Properly. With our hearts as well as our bodies. No more secrets, no more uncertainty—you do realize I'm a nervous wreck?'

Her gorgeous mouth dimpled at the corners, then

curved into a smile. 'Yes, Gavin. I would love to marry you properly.'

'Heaven help me,' he said huskily, staring at her mouth, 'I'll never get enough of you, Jo.'

'I think the same could be said of me!'

Later, he untied the sash of her pyjama top and told her she was extremely well dressed for what he had in mind.

She lay in his arms and chuckled. 'Just be careful of all the grazes and bruises.'

He lifted his head from her breasts. 'Damn, I'd forgotten!'

'Perhaps we could work out a plan whereby they might be avoided?' she suggested.

'A plan?' He scratched his head. 'How?'

'You're the ex-SAS person in the family, and pretty good at that,' she reminded him gravely. 'You've saved my life twice now.'

He grinned, then sobered. 'Would this fall into that category, by any chance?'

'Definitely. How about you?' she teased.

'If only you knew. Uh—well, a full inspection is certainly called for. That's basic SAS training, incidentally. Assess the situation thoroughly.'

'Oh, I'm all in favour of basic SAS training,' she said with a dreamy little smile. 'When do you plan to begin the assessment?'

'I could kiss you again first,' he offered, but they were both laughing and they came together in love and a mental unity that was breathtaking.

Several days later when they were back on Kin Can, Jo showed Gavin his portrait for the first time, his second portrait.

He stared at it. 'But this—this is different.'

'I know. This is the one I've worked on ever since you asked me to marry you, the first time.'

He studied it soberly. The inside of the old boundary hut was almost alive with the glow of firelight, and he was seated at the table, with a gun in his hands and naked to the waist.

'Jo—why?' he queried.

'I told you once, bone structure, muscles—all that is grist to my mill and you're a particularly fine specimen.'

'Is that all?'

'Well, no,' she conceded gravely. 'I wanted a reminder of my very own bushranger.'

He lifted an eyebrow. 'Even one who accused you of being a gangster's moll?'

She nodded.

'Do you plan to exhibit this?'

'Oh, no. Mind you, that's a pity. Even if I say so myself, it's some of my best work.'

'What do you plan to do with it?'

'Hang it up in our bedroom so even when you're away from me I can fantasize about you.'

He took a sudden breath. 'Do you have any idea what that will do to me?'

'Bring you home to me PDQ?' she suggested.

He put the picture down carefully and shook his head. 'You may find you have to prise me away with a crowbar, my lovely Jo.'

'Even better.' She moved into his arms. 'You haven't told me what you think of it.'

He looked across at the portrait. 'Well, I'm actually extremely taken with it.'

'Think you come across as a good-looking guy, or artistically?'

He wrapped his hands around her hips. 'Both.'

'You don't have to humour me.'

'Then—' his eyes softened '—artistically, it's so—I don't know how to put it into words—but it took me right back to the old hut. I could smell the wood smoke for a moment.'

She smiled. 'Thanks.'

'On the other hand, I don't know about the good-looking guy bit, but so long as I'm the guy you fantasize about—I really, truly, madly, deeply—appreciate that.'

Deep satisfaction filled Jo and she raised her mouth for his kiss.

RUTHLESS

Men who can't be tamed…or so they think!

If you love strong, commanding men, you'll love
this brand-new miniseries.

Meet the hard-edged, handsome, rich and rakish man
who breaks the rules to get exactly what he wants.
He's ruthless!

THE HIGH-SOCIETY WIFE

by Helen Bianchin

In Helen Bianchin's latest story, Gianna and
Franco Giancarlo are locked in a convenient society
marriage. Now Gianna has fallen in love with
her ruthless husband!

On sale this February.

THE
ELLIOTTS
Mixing business with pleasure

The saga continues this February with

Taking Care
of Business

by
Brenda Jackson

They were as different as night and day.
But that wouldn't stop Tag Elliott from
making it his business to claim the only
woman he desired.

**Available this February from
Silhouette Desire.**

HARLEQUIN®
Presents®

The world's bestselling romance series...
The series that brings you your favorite authors,
month after month:

Helen Bianchin...Emma Darcy
Lynne Graham...Penny Jordan
Miranda Lee...Sandra Marton
Anne Mather...Carole Mortimer
Susan Napier...Michelle Reid

and many more uniquely talented authors!

Wealthy, powerful, gorgeous men...
Women who have feelings just like your own...
The stories you love, set in exotic, glamorous locations...

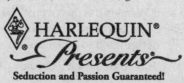

HARLEQUIN®
Presents®

Seduction and Passion Guaranteed!

From reader-favorite

Kathie DeNosky

THE ILLEGITIMATE HEIRS

A brand-new miniseries about three brothers denied a father's name, but granted a special inheritance.

Don't miss:

Engagement between Enemies

(Silhouette Desire #1700, on sale January 2006)

Reunion of Revenge

(Silhouette Desire #1707, on sale February 2006)

Betrothed for the Baby

(Silhouette Desire #1712, on sale March 2006)

HARLEQUIN *Presents*

The Arranged Brides

Settling a score—and winning a wife!

Don't miss favorite author Trish Morey's brand-new duet

PART ONE: STOLEN BY THE SHEIKH

Sapphire Clemenger is designing the wedding gown for Sheikh Khaled Al-Ateeq's chosen bride. Sapphy must accompany the prince to his exotic desert palace, and is forbidden to meet his future wife. She begins to wonder if this woman exists....

**Part two: The Mancini Marriage Bargain
Coming in March 2006**

www.eHarlequin.com

HPTAB0206